From What's Broken

Table of Contents

Part One
Amanda

1

"I want a divorce." The words slipped out in a stream of gloom and ambiguity.

My husband, Matthew, glanced away, his mouth tight and his eyes constricted. He had no words, but I wasn't surprised. We stared at each other like two strangers, two entirely different people—cold, distant, and doing what we needed to do in order to survive.

The decision hadn't come easy for me. For weeks, the idea of putting this limbo to rest had been on my mind. I couldn't live like this. Neither of us was happy.

"Did you hear me?" I whispered. I knew he had, but I needed confirmation. I needed some kind of response. Sad, happy, or mad, I didn't really care, but he owed it to me. He owed me a response.

"Yeah." He hugged his legs and glared past my gaze to the wall behind me. His eyes looked dead, calculating, and cold. Much of how they had been for most of the past year.

The hollowness returned. My heart gaped opened, threatening to swallow me entirely. Matthew and I blamed each other for Ivory's death. Now, nine months later, we stared at the end of our marriage. How or why did it have to come to this point?

In the back room, my other—rather, my *only*—daughter, Joy, began to cry. I didn't move. My body had become resistant to the sound of a baby. I held my stomach, my mind floundering.

I had still been pregnant with Joy when her sister was

taken from us. Soon Joy's cries turned into high-pitched wailing, yet I remained immobilized.

"Amanda, are you going to get her?" Matthew asked softly, still refusing to meet my gaze.

I bit my lip. I wanted to ask him what was wrong with his arms and legs, but I didn't. I turned and headed for the nursery across from our master bedroom. Stopping, I glanced into the room. The sheets remained scrunched at the bottom of the bed, our old, gray and black comforter thrown halfway to the floor. Gray and black—like everything in my life these days. Neither of us had slept in that bed in weeks. Matthew slept on the couch, and I slept on the daybed in the nursery.

Joy sobbed harder. I broke out of my stupor, entered her room, and picked her up. After a minute of rocking, her wailing softened to little cries. "There, there," I crooned. I shifted her in my arms so that we made eye contact. My stomach twisted in a terrible combination of admiration and disgust. She looked like Ivory did as a baby, but she had Matthew's eyes. I forced a smile, and she smiled back. Then I nursed her. When she fell asleep, I laid her softly in her crib.

I left the room, carefully closing the door, and returned to the living room. Matthew lay on the couch, his arms dangling to his side, his stare fixated on the ceiling. He was thinking, I could tell. I glared at him, wondering what he was thinking about. Was he thinking about what I had said? A divorce would be the perfect escape—for both of us. My heart sank. I felt like I had no choice. He wasn't going to pull the plug, yet our hearts were elsewhere.

I retrieved my car keys from the hook. I needed some

space to think and for my soon-to-be ex-husband to come to terms with what I had said.

"There is some breast milk in the fridge," I announced.

"Where are you going?"

I shrugged. "Why do you care?"

Matthew didn't respond and instead rolled over, his back to me.

I sighed. "It's for the best."

He didn't make a sound.

I turned to walk for the front door but stopped to look in his general direction. "There's breast milk in the fridge," I repeated just to make a point.

No response.

"Did you hear me?"

"Yeah." He jumped off the couch. "Have fun with your boss—I mean, *Roger*." There was a deadly edge to his voice.

This time it was my turn to respond with silence. I slammed the door behind me as hard as I could. *Screw him!*

2

I could hardly keep my eyes open. Today was the third day of no sleep and the baby fighting a vile cold and a minor fever. The only person she wanted was me. She didn't want her daddy, who, two weeks previous, had abandoned us to move in with his girlfriend, Rebecca — the same woman he had left me for in the first place. Now, she had *officially* claimed her place in Matthew's heart and bed.

He was supposed to have taken the baby for the night so I could catch up on sleep, but he called me an hour into his visit and said he couldn't deal with Joy's crying.

"What should I do?" he asked me.

I sighed and told him to drop her off at my place. I had accepted early on that he didn't want our baby to hinder his precious life with Rebecca. What happened to the loving father he once had been? I deemed that part of him had died with our first daughter.

As soon as he dropped her off, Joy nursed for what felt like forever. I held her. Her little cheeks blushed a deep red — the perfect shade of a tomato — and the heat of her fever burned against my breast as she ate. Eventually, she closed her eyes, which were puffy and red from crying. All I could do was comfort her.

"I love you," I told her.

She opened her eyes for a moment, stopped feeding, and smiled before restarting. My voice was a sense of comfort for her. This was all I could do for her for now. I wasn't a miracle worker.

My gaze drifted to the clock hanging above the crib. The second hand seemed to tick slowly and mechanically.

Tick.

Tick.

Tick.

It'd be another lonely, sleepless night. I'd be lucky to get a few hours of sleep before I had to go to work at the call center. My work consisted of demanding money from already-struggling people. It made my heart bleed, even if the mismanagement of their money was their own doing. But I guess work was better than staring at these four walls. This house was no longer my home. It had become a dungeon, a horrible reminder of every damn thing wrong with my life.

My face grew warm. I looked down at Joy and counted. "One. Two. Three." I needed to keep it together. "Four. Five. Six." My heartbeat settled, and the tension consuming me slowly vanished. "Seven. Eight. Nine. Ten." I took a deep breath and exhaled.

Life would go on.

I placed Joy in her crib and slipped out of her bedroom. I plopped on the couch in the living room, which still had lingering traces of Matthew's favorite cologne. He always had great taste in fragrances even if he wouldn't admit it. My gaze narrowed. Even though I had initiated the divorce, the separation had been harder than I thought it'd be.

I yawned. My eyelids felt heavy. The lack of sleep consumed me, threatening to swallow me whole. Between work and taking care of Joy, I had spent every spare moment mourning for my other daughter. I wasn't thriving but rather simply surviving the agonizing loss. I could barely sleep, eat, or function properly. She was always on my mind. That fateful day continued to haunt me. I closed my eyes, damming the wave of tears threatening to stream down my cheeks.

It had all happened so fast. I thought Matthew was watching her, so I slipped inside to make her a snack. Only, he thought I was watching her when he walked around to the other side of the house. It happened so, so fast. I didn't want to remember. I would never rid myself of the image of her laying in the street, the car screeching around the corner to escape that nightmare of a scene. Ivory was left gasping for air as the life drained from her blue eyes. I had raced outside and held her in those last moments, but I couldn't save her. I couldn't do anything for her.

I opened my eyes, and as I knew they would, the tears ran down my cheeks.

Why? Why had I felt the need to go inside the house? I thought Matthew had been watching her. Why on earth did he leave her alone in the front yard?

My mind replayed that terrible moment over and over again like a scene from a horror movie. I had only been inside the house for one minute. One fucking minute. But one minute had been enough time for her to run into traffic.

I crawled into a fetal position and allowed myself to bawl. The screeching of tires was embedded in my mind, accompanied by her gut-wrenching cry.

"Why did you have to die? Why, Ivory? Why?" I yelled to the empty room.

She had died en route to the hospital. The EMTs said

she never had a chance.

She never made it to her fourth birthday.

A piece of me died with her that day.

She should be alive, running around, playing with dolls, and dressing up in my oversized shirts and shoes. She was supposed to be there when I brought her sister home from the hospital.

A powerful wave of pain pierced my body. I tore at my hair as I tried to erase the image from my mind.

If only Matthew had been watching her. Now, here I was drowning in sorrow while he spent time with his lover. I yearned to wake from this nightmare, but the house had lost its vibrancy; instead, silence and the cold hands of death encompassed it. Ivory's passing was a reality I would not recover from. I had to accept that she was gone and would never return.

Joy cried once again from the back room. I wished she would sleep. She always needed me. Ivory had been such an easy baby. She had slept through the night at six-weeks-old and rarely cried. I could count on one hand how many times she was sick in her short life. Joy was anything but. She always had a cold or an earache and constantly wanted to be held. I should be excited that I had a child who wanted to be snuggled all the time, but I was so depressed.

I picked her up to comfort her. She smiled. All she needed was her mommy. I took her into the living room and laid her on the floor. Almost immediately, she raised herself onto her hands and knees. She would be crawling soon.

I smirked. "You can't wait until you can get into everything, isn't that right, Joy?"

Joy cooed as she flexed her chunky legs.

I got down and lay beside her, eye to eye. "You would've been so lucky to have Ivory as a big sister. She was so excited for your arrival."

Joy cooed louder.

I leaned over and kissed her on the forehead. "It's been a tough year, Joy. But it'll get better. I know it will."

I just wished her dad would have been here for us, but he wasn't. Eleven years together, gone, just like that.

I left Joy on the floor as I sat on the couch, retrieving my phone from the end table. I had three missed texts.

One from Matthew. *How is Joy doing?*

She is feeling better. She just woke up and is happy for now, I replied.

I clicked out of his name to check the next message.

Mom had texted me. *How are you doing today?*

Mom had been the only one there for me after Ivory's passing. I don't know what I would have done without her. I quickly typed a response. *It's been one of those days, Mom. I've been thinking a lot about Ivory. I'm trying to keep myself busy. Don't worry about me. I love you mom.*

The final text was from my boss, Roger. *How are you doing, lovely? Xoxo I've been thinking of you.* A big red heart punctuated the end of the message.

I responded with the same big heart and typed, *Not too bad. Just hanging out with Joy. And you?*

A few minutes later, he replied. *I thought her dad was watching her.*

I sighed. *He was supposed to be. But she has a cold and he couldn't handle it.*

Matthew's name came across the screen just then. *I'm*

taking the day off work tomorrow. I can take her for the day if you want.

I stared at the screen, debating how to respond. He was supposed to keep her for the afternoon today, not tomorrow. Six hours, three days a week is what we had agreed on until she weaned. He had already bailed on her once. Could I count on him? Then again, having him watch her would save money on hiring a private sitter since she couldn't attend daycare while she was sick.

Okay, can you pick her up by seven tomorrow? I typed. *I have to be at work by 8.*

I know your schedule. I'll be sure to pick her up. You can get her after you're done at work.

Okay.

I clicked out of his name and returned to my conversation with Roger.

Would you like some company? he had texted.

I smiled. *Yes.*

This was what I liked about my arrangement with Roger. It was innocent fun, a distraction from my shitty life. There were no strings attached, and it was therapeutic. It gave me a sense of comfort my husband couldn't give me anymore.

I'll see you soon. But I can't stay long.

Roger would never admit he was married, but I suspected he was. He didn't reveal too much information about his personal life, and I didn't ask.

I rushed to get Joy ready for bed. I changed her, fed her a quick bottle of breast milk from the fridge, and set her in her crib. I turned on her mobile, hoping it'd keep her occupied until she fell asleep. I dimmed the lights and slipped out of her room.

I walked into the bedroom and quickly picked up the sheets, haphazardly making the bed. I changed into a low-cut blouse and a loose skirt. I brushed my hair and spread a shade of crimson on my lips. I needed to appear somewhat put together for his arrival. I glanced in the mirror and noticed I still looked awful, so I finished by applying some eye drops. At least that made me look like I didn't just get done with one of my usual cry fests.

I waited in the living room and paced. Any minute, Roger would be here, and he'd temporarily fill the gaping hole in my heart Matthew had left. To drown out the silence, I turned on the antique radio Matthew had bought me years ago. I always liked old things. Over the years, I had inherited my grandparents' antique clock—which collected dust in my bedroom—a spoon collection that an old neighbor had given me before she passed, and several other antique trinkets steeped in history and sentimentality.

I glanced out the window as Roger pulled up in a rusted old pickup truck. It wasn't his usual sport utility vehicle he often drove to work, but I assumed he likely didn't want to be spotted driving his primary car outside his mistress's house.

That was a title I wasn't particularly proud of. After Matthew had reconnected with his ex, I grew lonelier, more scared, and I felt like I had no choice but to look for comfort elsewhere. My stomach recoiled. Matthew should have been there for me. I was the one who was pregnant. We had just lost a child. But he was too busy fulfilling his own selfish needs. Then Roger was there. He said all the right things. He *did* all the right things. The affair had really taken off after Joy was born—after Matthew had completely, without a doubt, checked out of our marriage. But in the back of my mind, I always wondered if Roger was married and if he was doing the same thing my husband was doing.

I bit my lip, shaking away the thoughts.

I watched him stop to glance in his side view mirrors, brushing his greyish hairs behind his ears. Today he wore a plain t-shirt and jeans—again, total opposite of his everyday work attire, which consisted of a button-up shirt and tie with freshly pressed slacks. He really did want to separate his professional life from his secret life with me.

I opened the door as he approached.

"Hey." He smirked as he walked past me into the porch area and kicked off his shoes into the corner. "The baby sleeping?"

"She's in her room, yeah."

He followed me into the living room.

"Can I get you anything to drink?" I asked.

"I'm good." He plopped onto my couch and propped his legs on the coffee table. He looked at me. "Mandy? Why don't you come and sit down?" He patted the couch beside him.

I did as he asked and sat beside him, our legs touching. He caressed my face, brushing away a few random strands of hair. He reached in and kissed me.

Wow, he isn't wasting any time.

"You look good tonight," he whispered in my ear.

I half-laughed. If one counted lack of sleep from a sick baby and a puffy face from crying from so much unspoken grief as attractive, then I guess I did win in that department.

He touched my bare thigh, and his fingers inched up my leg. "Loosen up, Mandy. You're so tense."

"I had a rough day."

He frowned for a moment, looking almost annoyed. His round blue eyes glistened. The blue eyes were the only resemblance I could find between Matthew and Roger. I purposely was attracted to Roger because he was so different from my husband.

"Let me make you feel better." Not waiting for a response, Roger kissed me on the neck.

Some of the built-up tension lessened as I reached for his pants and loosened the top button.

"That a girl." He licked his lips. He made no secret of his intentions.

I reached over and kissed him. Right now, was as good of a time as ever. We didn't know how long Joy would be asleep, and frankly, I needed a break from the everyday reminder of life.

Roger kissed me back as he undressed me. Then, right there on the living room floor, we had silent sex. When he finished, a satisfied smile crossed his face. I tried to smile, but I felt empty. Even the pleasure he tried to give me didn't put a dent in my grieving soul. Yet I said nothing. I let him have his way anyway. I opened my mouth to speak, to tell him I wanted more, but I didn't. It wasn't his problem if I didn't get what I sought from our arrangement. And that was all it was—an arrangement.

He stood and retrieved his clothing strewn along the room. "I must be going. I have to work tomorrow."

I wished he'd stay for a bit longer. I wanted him to ask me how I felt, even if only from the place of a caring friend.

"Have a good night," I said and turned to collect my clothes.

He approached me once more, and we kissed. "Have a good night, Mandy."

I waited as he let himself out.

In and out.

I sat up and hugged my legs. I knew I should be used to this arrangement. It was for the best, but sometimes I wished for a little more. I missed the connection.

***

The following morning, my alarm vibrated at 6:30, not that I required the reminder. I didn't sleep well anyway. If I didn't have a baby to pay attention to or a job to attend, I'd waste the whole day in bed, sealing myself from the outside world. I glanced into the crib where Joy was awake and infatuated with the wooden mobile Matthew had made for her. When she spotted me, she sported a big gummy smile. I picked her up and started to change her.

"Daddy's going to spend the day with you today," I told her in my high-pitched happy talk.

Joy murmured.

"I'm sure your daddy misses you so much." I teared up as I finished fastening the fresh nappy and reached for a clean onesie.

Joy cooed again. We both missed her daddy, but it was for the best.

"I'll pick you up after work, I promise." I bent down

and kissed the soft skin of her belly.

Joy, at least, slept better last night, and her cheeks weren't as crimson as they were the day before. That was marvelous news. I settled on a frilly skirt to complete her outfit. I carried her to the living room and plunked her into her bouncer in front of the television. It'd at least provide a temporary distraction if I was lucky.

I strolled into my bedroom to get ready for the day and sighed. Why couldn't I just sleep the day away? On my nightstand was a picture of Matthew, Ivory, and me. It should have been all four of us — Matthew, Ivory, Joy, and me. We had planned this baby, and now our family was split in two. Neither of us was the attentive, loving parent Joy deserved.

I shook my head and grabbed something to wear. I didn't even care what, as long as it was clean. Upon looking in the mirror, I realized I looked like I had gotten ready with my eyes closed. Today would be just another day, and I needed to get through it. That was what I told myself. It was all I could say.

I threw my hair into a ponytail and headed for the living room to wait for Matthew to pick up the baby. There was some expressed breast milk in the fridge. I just hoped there was enough. Joy had been nursing a lot more lately, and I wasn't sure if her dad was pace feeding her. He never understood the concept, even when Ivory was alive, but he did it regardless. He was always a good listener. Or at least he used to be.

I waited in the living room, crossed-legged on the floor. Goosebumps scattered my arms. I didn't look forward to seeing him. Whenever he came, and every time he left, sadness consumed me.

My cell phone, charging on the end table, blinked.

Be there in 5, Matthew texted.

Okay, I replied.

I stood and headed to the kitchen, retrieving the few bottles I had pumped throughout the night, and put them in the diaper bag. I added a few extra diapers and a change of clothes.

A bitter taste filled my mouth. My daughter growing up in two households was never my goal for her. I never wanted this, any of this.

I'm sorry, Joy.

Matthew knocked on the door before he let himself in. I wanted to tell him he didn't live here anymore, even if his name was still on the deed. He was the one who left.

I stopped and glanced at him. He donned the red wool sweatshirt I had bought him for his birthday last year, and he wore the same cologne he always did. He held onto the doorknob as he rubbed his other hand through his unkempt, shaggy brown hair. He hadn't shaved in a week. I was amazed at how he had really let himself go—but then again, I knew I didn't look the part of a prim-and-proper functioning member of society either. Maybe he was feeling as shitty as I felt. But at least he had Rebecca's soft touch.

I was grateful he hadn't brought Rebecca.

"Is Joy ready?"

I nodded, handing him the bag. "If she runs out of breast milk, just give her formula."

He pressed his fist against his chest and opened his mouth to speak but changed his mind. "Okay."

"What were you going to say?"

"Nothing," he mumbled.

I placed my hands on my hips. "Don't tell me 'nothing.' What were you going to say?"

He sighed and looked me dead in the eyes. "You knew I was coming, so there's no reason why you shouldn't have more than enough breast milk for the baby."

I swallowed hard, my chin trembling.

He threw up his hands. "See, that's why I didn't want to say anything. I didn't want to hurt your feelings."

"That's wonderful, Matthew, because you never cared about my feelings at all for the last year."

He gazed downward before making eye contact with me again. "I'm sorry, okay, Ma— Amanda. I have to go."

I missed the days when he called me Mandy. Now I was just Amanda.

I retrieved Joy and kissed her on the forehead. "Have a good day with Daddy, Joy."

Matthew smiled briefly but frowned just as quickly. "Pick her up when you're done working."

"I will." I wanted to roll my eyes. As if I could forget we had a daughter together, no matter how much I wanted to.

Without another word, he headed out the door with Joy and diaper bag in hand.

I glanced through the screen door, watching him buckle her into the back seat. He didn't even glance my way as he got into the driver's seat and drove away.

Would this be how divorce looked? Would the hurt of watching him drive away with Joy for his parenting time ever disappear? Would I have to endure the awkward arguments much longer? When we got married, never in a million years did we expect this. But here we were.

3

A month had passed since Matthew moved out, so it should have been easier on me, but my fists still shuddered as I made my way to meet him.

"Can we meet for coffee to discuss some things?" he had asked. I knew what he wanted to talk about — divorce. We had talked little about the end of our marriage, at least not since I pulled the plug. But seeing him neatly pack his t-shirts and belongings — many of which I had bought for him over the years — into suitcases almost brought me to my knees.

I was so furious with him in the beginning. "If you want *her* so badly, why don't you just leave?" I had told him, but a part of me hoped him to stick around. When he left, I didn't foresee it to be so hard. The night before he officially moved into Rebecca's one-bedroom condo, we didn't exchange more than a few words. I was invisible to him. He tried to load the living room television into his SUV, but I told him he couldn't. He didn't put up a fight. Instead, he mumbled, "I'll be out of your hair soon."

He hadn't taken a single family-photo, not even one of Ivory or Joy as if he wanted to dispose of his memories of us from his life. Not taking any photos of me, I understood, but even his children? Ivory may no longer be with us, but she was still our daughter.

I sat in my car in the parking lot at work, staring at the message from him for a while before I finally grew the courage to reply. *Where do you want to meet? Somewhere by the daycare. I have until six to pick her up. That gives us a little over an hour.*

I stared at my phone, waiting for his response.

The coffee shop on the corner is fine. See you soon.

I slowly steered the car from the curb, filled with dread. Up until a year ago, we looked forward to meeting one another in the middle of the workday. I always had little butterflies fluttering around in my chest. He used to be able to sweep me off my feet. His smile and scent made me go wild. Now I felt nothing but foreboding at the thought of having to sit down with him.

I passed the preschool Ivory had attended for a few short months. Matthew and I had both taken that morning off from work to bring her to the first day of school. I inhaled hard and my shoulders convulsed as I recalled the day. Joy had been the complete opposite. She didn't get the recognition we both had given Ivory. Even on the day she was born, her father showed up three hours after I was admitted. He was there for her birth, but I suffered through most of the labor without my husband. I didn't know where he had been, and he said he had stayed late at work, but I speculated he had been with Rebecca. I couldn't prove it. It didn't matter. He wasn't there for me when he was physically there. I pulled up to the coffee shop. Matthew was already standing by the door, still dressed in his suit and tie. He leaned against the brick building, sporting a blank stare. He stood upright when he saw me approach.

"Hi!" I said, trying to smile.

He remained standing several feet from me. "Hi, Amanda."

We stood in silence for a few moments, simply staring

at one another. He had nothing to say — so typical of Matthew.

I heaved a breath. "Shall we go in?"

He couldn't even show any emotion. He couldn't ask me how I was or ask how Joy was. Nothing. Instead, I was welcomed with indifference. He was cold. He was not the man I had married. He was a complete stranger.

I gnawed at my upper lip. I couldn't let him get under my skin. Our marriage was dead, and I'd never have the man I fell in love with back.

I followed him inside. He approached the counter and ordered a coffee before standing to the side. I did the same, and we sat down at a table in the far corner of the shop.

My legs trembled. "How have you been?" I asked, instantly regretting the question.

"I'm good. And you?"

"All right." I wanted to tell him that I was miserable. I wanted to tell him how he wasn't there for me and Joy. But I didn't. What would have been the point?

Matthew took a swig of his beverage. "I was hoping we could handle things amicably."

I nodded. I knew the topic of divorce would come up. "Okay."

"I know this is hard for you, but I don't want to make things drag out any longer."

My mouth twisted. "So, you feel nothing? This isn't hard for you at all?" I didn't yell, but in that moment, I could have cut the tension with a knife.

Matthew rubbed the back of his neck and glanced away for a moment. "None of this is easy, Amanda. But remember, you — "

"What choice did I have?" My heart rate accelerated, and an uncontrollable rage built in my core. "Did you expect us to continue living the way we were?"

Matthew put one finger to his mouth, shushing me. "I don't want to fight with you."

I took a deep breath, preventing myself from further blowing up on him. "Fine!"

Matthew rubbed the nape of his neck again. "It isn't easy for any of us. Please, let's make this as easy as possible."

I bowed my head. "All right." I told myself I wouldn't react, but it was so hard.

"Okay, first of all, the house."

I stared at him. "What about the house?"

He glared back at me. "We need to talk about how to divide up the house. Either we sell it and split the profits or you buy me out."

A sudden, heavy grief emerged inside me. I didn't want to uproot Joy from the house, but I could never afford it on my own. Matthew had paid the mortgage this month, but I couldn't expect him to continue paying for it.

"I guess we sell it. You know I can't afford it." My eyes became wet with tears, and I stood. "I can't talk about this right now. I'll call you later, Matthew."

"Come on, no time will be a good time. I just want to put this behind us."

I sat back down. "You just want to pretend the last year didn't happen."

His fist clenched. "I'll never forget about Ivory. How dare you say otherwise!"

I looked away and mumbled an insincere apology. He

wasn't there for me then, and he wasn't now. He wanted to forget all about us. That was the truth.

"Enough of this, Amanda!" His voice rose. Other customers began turning toward us, and he realized how loud he was being. He instantly lowered his voice. "Let's just talk business, okay? We'll sell the house, split the equity."

"Fine," I mumbled. I didn't want to talk about the house anymore. I couldn't think about packing everything into boxes and crates, and I didn't want to talk to him at all either.

"Now, about Joy."

I shrugged. "What's there to talk about? We already agreed to six hours, three days a week for you. She's nursing and needs her mother."

He bit his lip. "That won't last forever. I'm talking long term."

I let out a long, low sigh. "When she weans." I didn't know why we were discussing this. We both wanted her to be on breast milk as long as possible. It had been his idea when we had Ivory, and he had intended to do the same for Joy.

"Can't you just pump more so I can have her on Saturdays? Maybe Sundays too, when I'm off?"

"That's unreasonable," I snapped immediately.

His lips pressed together in a slight grimace. "I just want a relationship with Joy."

"Who said you couldn't have one? Now who's making this personal?"

"You won't discuss custody with me. *You're* making this personal, Amanda."

I swallowed a few times before speaking again. "It was you who wanted me to breastfeed the kids. Joy is only eight months old, so give it a bit longer, okay?"

I kept darting my eyes toward the door. Matthew was getting under my skin. He knew how to push my buttons, and I felt the urge to reach across the table and slap him. I wasn't a violent person. He wasn't thinking of Joy, and it made me furious. I'd bet anything that Rebecca was chirping in his ear back at their place. He changed after the two of them had reconnected. He became an inconsiderate ass. I guess tragedy brought out the worst in people, myself included. "We don't need to talk about it right now," he conceded, staring at his lap.

"Good. Now, is there anything else you want to talk about?"

He sighed but didn't say anything.

"Why don't we talk about debt?" If he wanted to talk business, we'd talk business.

He looked up at me. "What debt?"

I folded my arms and leaned back in my seat. "There's my car loan, which you are the cosigner for, and the joint credit card."

His posture tightened. "That's *your* debt."

I shrugged. "Maybe so, but your name is on the deed, and the debt was accumulated during the course of our marriage. You want this to be a clean and *fair* divorce. So, you better start thinking fairly or things could get expensive."

"Why are you acting this way, Mandy?"

I looked at my phone. It was almost time to pick up Joy.

I chugged the rest of my now lukewarm beverage. "I've got to go, all right? I have to go pick up *our* daughter. Why don't you make a list of what you think is fair, and I'll do the same? Then we'll meet again and compare, all right?"

Without waiting for a response, I rose from my seat and exited the building. I couldn't deal with him right now. It was too hard.

The instant the cold air hit my face, tears welled in my eyes. How did it come to this? I leaned against the building, struggling to maintain my composure.

Matthew came out the door and approached me. "What was that in there?" The lines in his face deepened into a frown. "Remember, this is what *you* wanted. *You* wanted to end our marriage."

I glared at him and opened my mouth. An insult was on the tip of my tongue, ready to be unleashed, but I stopped myself and instead asked, "Are you saying you want to stay married?"

Matthew gazed downward.

I stared right at him. "Were you happy?" I already knew the answer, but I didn't think it was fair for him to put all this on me. "Be honest with yourself. You were waiting for me to pull the plug so that you could feel better about yourself."

"No, I haven't been happy. Is that what you want to hear?"

"It's been a hard year. Ever since the accident. I didn't know what else to do." Tears rained down my cheeks. "I-I miss her. I-I …" I miss us, our family, I wanted to say but couldn't.

Matthew turned away. "Me too, Mandy. Me too."

I glanced at my phone. "I have to pick up Joy. We'll talk about this another time."

"Okay," Matthew replied as he drew a deep breath. "Have a good night, Amanda."

"You too."

We walked our separate ways, and I got into my car. I glanced out the window as I watched him cross the street. At the corner, he stopped short of his SUV and stared at it before turning and walking to the tavern. He went inside. It must be nice to drink away the pain.

I sighed heavily and pulled away from the curb and headed for the daycare. I had to accept that life would go on. I'd be a single, divorced mother, grieving the loss of my daughter, the loss of my marriage, and the loss of my best friend—my partner in crime.

I pulled up in front of the daycare and shot a quick text to Roger. *What are you doing tonight? In about an hour or so.*

I exited my vehicle and headed toward the entrance. Life went on. That was what I had to tell myself day in and day out.

Ariel, the mother of another one of the kids, approached me with a smile. "Hello, Amanda. How are you doing?"

"I'm doing fine. And you?" I lied. I didn't want to tell her my life was shit.

"Just picking up Elizabeth and heading home to make supper."

"Same."

We didn't say much more. I followed her into the daycare. A staff member greeted us and chitchatted with

Ariel while we waited for them to deliver our kids.

When they returned with Joy, she had a big smile plastered across her face.

I smiled. "Hey, sweetie."

She cooed. At least she was happy.

"She had a good day," the daycare worker said. They handed me her diaper bag, and I left.

After I buckled Joy into her seat, I checked my messages.

I can't get away until close to 9, Roger had texted.

That's fine! I replied.

I drove to the nearest fast-food restaurant. I didn't feel like cooking. I didn't really feel like eating anything at all, but I knew I needed to maintain my strength. I needed to keep it together for Joy.

I ordered tacos. It had been months since I last had tacos. They were one of the staple foods I used to make. Ivory would demand them at least once a week. I used to make the shells from scratch, but I hadn't had the heart to make them since. Avoiding any memory of her was one way to keep my grief at bay.

I sat in the parking lot, staring at my order like it was a foreign object. Slowly, I forced the chicken taco down my throat. The flavors were good, but I had little appetite. Thick bile accumulated in my throat. Joy fussed in the back seat, which was my signal to stop eating and head home. I needed to get her ready for bed and get myself together for Roger.

By the time I pulled into the driveway, Joy had fallen asleep. I didn't move though. I stared at the mid-century house. I had fallen in love with this house — both Matthew and I had. It was love at first sight, just like when we had met, or so I thought. Sooner or later, someone else would own it. It'd be just one more thing to add to the list of things I had lost. I might as well start looking at apartments to move into. Something I could afford on my salary alone. The joint debt we had accumulated would most likely deplete any money I should receive from the house in the split. It was a sad reality I had to accept.

I got out of the car and took Joy inside. I changed her into her pajamas and nursed her. Providing Joy with natural food was the least I could do for her until I could get my own emotions in check. I had breastfed Ivory until she was almost two, but knew I wouldn't be able to do the same with Joy. Matthew would never accept the current arrangement for another sixteen months, and I couldn't afford a lawyer to fight him. I didn't have the strength or desire to decimate what little respect we still had for one another.

I put Joy in her bouncer before heading to the bathroom to shower. Sweaty, I soon realized I hadn't showered at all in the past few days. I guess life happened. At least Joy had gotten over her latest cold, but it was only a matter of time before she would become sick again.

I turned on the shower and let the hot stream drench me from head to toe as my mind wandered. Soon Roger would be here to make me feel better. Matthew was out finding relief at the bottom of a bottle. I deserved to find comfort, too, even if it was from Roger. I hoped he would stick around a bit longer today.

It was hit or miss with him. Sometimes, he'd stay for a few hours. We'd talk, do the deed, and watch some television. Other times, it was in and out—no strings attached. I couldn't let myself get dependent on him. It was less complicated that way.

I got out of the shower and changed into a t-shirt and short-shorts. Today I didn't look like I had just rolled out of bed, so I didn't feel the need to plaster on makeup. I sat beside Joy, who was watching a children's television show. I blocked out the noise and watched the brightly colored characters sing their annoying songs. Joy loved it.

I'll be there in 10 minutes, Roger texted.

OK, I replied.

I turned off the television and put Joy to bed.

Pacing the hallway, I waited for him to arrive. When he did, my heart skipped a beat. I just hoped he would stay longer tonight. I needed the comfort, after today.

He brought a case of beer with him when he came to the door. I was in luck, he likely wasn't in any hurry.

He smiled warmly when he saw my face. "I thought you could use a distraction. The boys at work said you looked preoccupied."

I nodded. "And I just got back from meeting Matthew."

He raised an eyebrow and allowed himself in. "About?"

"We were discussing the divorce. I need to start looking for a place to live."

Roger cracked open a beer and took a swig. "You should talk to a lawyer, Mandy." He reached into the case and handed me one.

I had some breast milk in the fridge, so I could get away with having one beer.

"Thanks."

He brushed some hair from my face. "Smile, Mandy. You glow when you smile."

I smiled. Matthew used to tell me I had a beautiful smile. At least someone else noticed it.

Roger reached in and kissed me. "You look mighty sexy," he whispered when we separated.

"You too."

He smirked. "If you say so. Care to show me?"

I chugged the rest of the beer in one gulp, reached in, and kissed him again. I proceeded to undress. At least he was here when I needed him.

When we finished, I lay back on the floor catching my breath. Roger smiled as he slowly got dressed.

"Feel better?" he asked.

"Yeah." I joined him in putting my clothes back on. "Are you planning on staying?" I tried to keep the hopeful tone out of my voice.

"For a little bit." He got up and headed into my kitchen. "Do you have anything to eat?"

"I have some chips in the cupboard."

"Good enough," he said, grabbing the bag and returning to the living room. He opened the bag and placed it on the coffee table.

I joined him on the couch.

"So, what do you have planned for the weekend?"

I thought for a moment. "I'll probably take Joy to see my mother in the morning, then drop her off with her dad."

"Would you be up for a quickie? Saturday's are usually pretty busy, but I can try to fit you in."

I bit my lip. "I'll text you Friday to let you know." It all depended on how I felt. While I enjoyed Roger's company, I was okay with simply being his booty call, just someone he'd fit into his day, like a doctor's appointment. I also planned on catching up on my sleep that day.

He reached over and kissed me again. "Sounds good, Mandy." He brushed the side of my face with his hand. "You really should loosen up some more."

I nodded. If only he knew. I bet he had never had to experience the loss of a child, and to top it off, have a spouse leave him for another person. And that person being his ex. Here I was, someone's sidepiece. The thought made me cringe even though I did consent to all this.

"You're so young, vibrant, and beautiful. Don't waste that." His words did boost my confidence. It was nice to know others still found me attractive. Heck, I hadn't been feeling desired lately. Rejected was more accurate.

Roger and I sat there making small talk, but Joy started to cry again. I sighed.

"I'll take that as my cue to head out. You take care." He reached over and kissed me one last time. I wanted him to stay.

When he let himself out, I dragged myself to the bedroom to take care of Joy. All I wanted was someone to talk to, some kind of adult interaction.

Joy was wide awake, grabbing at her feet when I went to pick her up.

"You really know how to pick bad times to need Mommy."

She giggled. I wasn't mad. I was her mom, and I needed to be there. She was all I had left, the only positive thing remaining in my life, the one thing that hadn't been taken from me. She deserved my attention, and I was happy to give it even if it came at a bad time.

I fed her a few ounces from the fridge. The beer I drank would be out of my system before her next feeding. She fell fast asleep soon after. In a few weeks, she'd be suffering from another growth spurt, so I might as well enjoy the longer stretches of napping.

Instead of sleeping on the daybed, I headed to my bedroom. I hadn't slept in my own bed in a while. Tonight, for some reason, I wanted to. I couldn't say why.

I changed into my pajamas and crawled into bed. Tomorrow was another day. I went to charge my phone when I noticed a notification. It was probably Roger texting me good night.

Instead, Matthew's name appeared on the screen.

I think about Ivory every single day. So, don't go thinking otherwise. For damn sakes UR making this harder than it needs to be. Today was supposed to be easy. Why can't you make things easy? Why can't you accept that I'm with Rebecca? I've accepted you luuvvv Roger. So why make this hard? Huh? Amanda!

There were several more texts from Matthew that included a vibrant vocabulary. I clenched my phone, ready to reply with something I would probably regret later, when I remembered he had been heading into the bar when we went our separate ways.

I set my alarm and went to sleep.

4

I pushed the stroller down the paved path by the river. The sun shone brightly, and the birds were chirping. Wild flowers waved in the breeze on either side of me. I came to an uneven trail leading to the cemetery — the cold, silent place we had laid Ivory to rest.

"Ready to visit your sister?" I asked Joy.

I sauntered through the rows of the deceased with my head lowered — all those whose souls had reached Heaven. I wasn't religious by any means, but I found comfort knowing Ivory was in Heaven looking over her sister. I had to believe that.

We reached Ivory's grave. Through our grief, Matthew and I had managed to keep it together enough to agree on where to bury her. Besides his mother and one brother, none of Matthew's family lived nearby, so we chose to lay Ivory near my grandmother who had passed shortly before she was born.

I brushed my hand along the tombstone. *Ivory Rose Talan, 2014 - 2018.* It was Matthews's idea to only include the years she was alive and omit the dates. She had been so excited for her birthday. She wanted to invite all her friends from school and have a lot of cake and balloons. It was all she talked about during the weeks leading to the accident. He wanted it to seem like she had made it to four years.

So, I agreed.

"How are you doing, sweetie?" I asked.

A strange aura surrounded me. I always felt like Ivory was trying to communicate with me when I was here, like I could connect with her spirit.

I took Joy out of the stroller and sat her next to a nearby tree and stared at the tombstone, watching Joy play in the grass. I just wanted to sit here and spend some time with Ivory, knowing, when I left her grave, the pain would hit me like a ton of bricks. For now, though, it was comforting. It helped to spend time with her.

"It's a nice day, isn't it?" I wasn't sure if I was speaking to Joy or to Ivory in particular, but Joy tutted.

At least someone is answering me, I thought.

Joy clasped her little fingers on a dandelion. She pulled, snapping the stem, and brought the weed straight to her mouth.

"No, no, Joy." I pulled her hand away from her mouth. "That's yuckies." I stuck out my tongue.

Joy mimicked me and laughed.

"You little turkey."

I checked my phone. Roger hadn't texted me in a few days. He was probably with his real family — the one he never talked about.

Matthew hadn't mentioned the divorce again either, so at least, that gave me some time before I had to settle. I had looked at apartments. Most of the ones near the daycare in my price range were small. I felt deflated when I thought about just how much my lifestyle was about to change — how Joy and I would have to live in a dingy, one-bedroom apartment or I'd have to live across town in a not-so-nice area, with the commute.

I stared at Joy, who had long since fallen asleep in my

lap. Her mouth was wide open, with her tongue stuck out. She slept so peacefully, something I missed so desperately. I leaned back, starting at the sky.

My phone rang. Matthew's number came across the screen.

I heaved a sigh and answered. "Hello."

"Where are you?"

"I'm not at home. Why?"

"I've been trying to text you for over an hour." I heard a long, drawn-out sigh on the other line.

"Okay, my phone was on silent. You have my attention, so what do you want?" I adjusted my position, careful not to wake Joy.

There was an awkward silence, with heavy breathing on the other end.

"What do you want, Matthew?" I bit my lip. "Just spit it out." Sometimes he would call and not say anything. He'd make me drag the information out of him.

"I-I know you don't want to talk about this but have you put any thought into what we talked about? I've given you a few weeks, but I really want to talk about it."

I gritted my teeth, my heartbeat racing. "I'm busy," I whispered. I held the phone, considering hanging up on him.

"Why are you making this hard?"

"I didn't say I wouldn't discuss it with you, but right now, I'm busy. Okay?"

"Are you busy with *Roger*?"

"Fuck off. If you must know, I'm at the cemetery visiting Ivory, unlike you. Now leave me alone."

This time I hung up on him. I held on to Joy, my

stomach twisting in knots. I stared at the tombstone again. "I don't like fighting with your dad, Ivory."

We used to be inseparable. The irony of the whole thing was nauseating.

We had met at a bar for a mutual acquaintance's birthday. I was there with a close male friend, whom I wasn't quite together with, but we were more than friends. It was complicated. Matthew was there with Rebecca. I gagged at just the thought of her name. But she was there and a part of his past and his present. I couldn't stand her.

I had gone to the bar to order a drink. I had just celebrated my birthday, and I still had that exciting feeling of being able to order at a bar just because I could. The best part was, I no longer had to sneak around whereas Matthew was six years older than me. That moment, I had gone to order myself a drink. When the bartender finished, I went to pay but couldn't find my wallet. I was tipsy, unsettled, and shy. That was when Matthew came up and paid for my drink while ordering for himself and Rebecca. We exchanged a few words, he smiled and returned to the table.

I sat beside my friend, where I had left my wallet inside my purse, and for the rest of the night, we stared at one another. Rebecca noticed and scowled at me. I remembered smiling back. It was kind of mean, but I was drunk, he had bought me a drink, and I appreciated him coming to my rescue.

A few weeks later, I met up with our mutual friend again. This time, I went alone, and he came alone. We were hanging out, eating, drinking beer, and playing blackjack. Nearing the end of the night, Matthew and I were talking.

He described his relationship with Rebecca as I kind of just sat there listening. He wasn't happy and wanted to break up with her. Turns out, two weeks later, they broke up, and our friend gave him my number.

We started texting, and the rest was history. I moved in with him after four months. We got engaged and got married after knowing each other only nine months. I've never forgotten the look on my mom's face when I told her we were engaged. She was in the kitchen preparing a chicken stew, wearing a red smock. "I'm getting married." Matthew and I were sitting on the couch.

"Don't you lie to me," she had said, staring and hoping we would break out laughing. But when we didn't, she frowned. "You're serious?"

We nodded, and Matthew stood to face her. "I promise to take care of her." He had looked her straight in her eye and promised.

That was the irony of things— he wasn't there for me. When I had needed him the most, he ran away. He ran back to Rebecca — the woman he had claimed he wasn't happy with. Was I surprised? He had left Rebecca so quickly and gotten with me. He could as soon dispose of me just as quickly. But I thought I was different because he had married me and not her, his first fiancée — the one he had left for me.

Joy woke up fussing. I nursed her and continued to just sit there numbed. I thought I'd be crying, thinking about rejection — about that woman being with Matthew. I didn't know if him being with any other woman was any different.

I checked my phone again. He had sent me a bunch of

texts just like he said.

Have you made your list yet? he had texted.

Nope, Matthew, I hadn't. I knew I should, but I didn't want to think about it. What I was entitled to and what I would ask for were two very different things.

Could you call your mom to babysit Joy for a bit, or I could ask Rebecca to watch her? I read another of his texts. My stomach recoiled. Joy was my daughter, and there was no way I wanted her around Rebecca more than I had to. I swallowed hard.

I swiped out of the messages. I couldn't take reading any of them. Maybe it would be better to contact a lawyer. Just thinking about discussing anything with him left me emotional and full of dread. I didn't trust Rebecca, and I feared he'd try to pull a fast one over me.

I lifted Joy, who was now awake, into a standing position. She smiled, and I smiled. I stood and brought her to the tombstone, the reason I came here in the first place.

"Do you hear her?" I asked. "Ivory, Joy's trying to speak with you."

I sat in silence as Joy cooed. Then laughed. Gurgled, and laughed some more. I knew she was speaking to her sister. Before Ivory had died, I never believed in ghosts or spirits. I had gained a new perspective, a new meaning to life I didn't know of before.

My mind floundered.

I had held on to Ivory on the street. *No!* I had screamed. I hadn't remembered who had called the police, but it wasn't long before red and blue lights surrounded the area. They had to peel me from her. "Don't take my baby from me." Matthew was shaking and holding me.

"It'll be okay!" he had said. He had said it a few times, but I didn't believe it. The ambulance had arrived and loaded her up. Matthew and I got into our car. The drive was the longest twenty minutes of our lives. Neither of us said a word in those twenty minutes leading through the doors of emergency and the doctor saying. *I'm sorry, she didn't make it.*

Tears fell down my face. "I'm sorry I wasn't there to stop you." I laid Joy on the grass on her belly, embracing the tombstone, letting the tears fall. "I'm so, so sorry, Ivory. If only your dad was watching, you. I just wanted to make you a snack. You were playing, and I thought you'd want something to eat. I was only gone a minute."

They said it'd get easier with time. They said the pain would lessen. They said I'd be able to move on. But, how could I? How could I move on without my baby girl?

His voice broke the dead silence of the cemetery. "Amanda?"

I couldn't bring myself to make eye contact. "What are you even doing here?"

Matthew remained silent for a moment. "Sorry. I guess we don't have to discuss it right this minute if you don't want to."

My chest ached. I struggled to swallow from the choking dryness of my throat. "No, you need to tell me what you're doing here. Why are you here?" I felt fleeting remorse for the acuity of my words, but I didn't want him here. I didn't want to share this precious alone time with the man who was never there for me when I needed him.

I stared as Matthew approached her headstone and placed a flower on her grave. He approached the stroller and picked up Joy. "Hey, baby girl. Here's my other little princess."

I heard sadness in his voice. With each wobble of his chest, I felt my heart ripped open yet again — the memory of the first time Matthew held Ivory in his arms and his tears of joy.

"Who's my baby girl?"

Ivory was only a few hours old. Matthew had rocked her while gazing into her sapphire-blue eyes. He kissed the tiny fingers wrapped around his thumb.

I retrieved Joy from Matthew's arm — "I can't do this" — and placed her in the stroller and turned to leave.

"Wait!" Matthew said.

I stopped and forced myself to look him in the eyes. "I can't do this."

"Don't go! Don't run away when things get tough."

"You're one to talk."

"I'm sorry, okay? This has been hard for the both of us."

A wave of sorrow overwhelmed me. My legs shook, and I felt faint. Matthew hesitated before approaching and wrapping his arms around me. I collapsed against his chest and sobbed until I could barely breathe. The image of her lying in the street came crashing back like a ton of bricks.

"Why did she have to die?" I gasped. "Why, Matthew? Why?"

"I-I don't know, Mandy. I don't know. I ask myself the same question every day."

After my sobs subsided into soft hiccupping, he released me.

I glanced at him. It was the first physical contact we'd

had in months. I was almost taken aback. In the first few weeks following Ivory's death, we clung to each other like sinking swimmers. After her funeral, we drifted apart.

I retrieved a tissue from the fanny pack around my waist and wiped my nose. When I saw the pain etched on Matthew's face, I sensed a familiar flutter in my chest.

"Despite what you may think," he said, "I think about Ivory every day. I see her face wherever I look. I dream about her at night."

I remorsefully glanced away. "I know you do." Locked in my pain and bitterness, I barely acknowledged his grief.

He took the crumpled tissue from my trembling hand and dabbed my eyes. "I don't want to keep fighting with you, Mandy. More than anything, I want you to be happy. You deserve that much."

I forced a weak smile. "You too, Matthew." I looked at Joy, asleep in her stroller, oblivious to the extreme grief from her parents a few feet away. "You want Joy for a few hours?"

Matthew frowned. His demeanor changed. "You want to spend time with someone?"

"Forget I asked," I said with a sigh. "I just thought maybe you'd want to be with your other daughter, but its fine."

Matthew shook his head and touched my shoulder. "I'm sorry. That was a stupid thing to say."

I took a deep, quaking breath. "If you care at all, Roger and I aren't in a relationship. We never were and never will be. It's just a distraction."

Matthew started to speak and then stopped.

"I'll text you tomorrow and let you know when to pick

up Joy for your parenting time." I took the stroller and walked away.

I didn't even say goodbye to Ivory or Matthew. I just couldn't. Matthew was with Rebecca, and that was the way it would have to stay.

I made the ten-minute walk home and lay on the couch. I wanted — no, I needed — to talk to my mom.

Mom, I need you.

5

I strolled through the front doors of the call center. Another day of work and another day of making those phone calls no one likes to receive, and if only they knew, calls most of us didn't want to make. However, it was still a job. I could never find anything substantial with the history degree the university had awarded me. Thankfully, I had that scholarship, or I'd be drowning in student loans I couldn't repay. I'd love to teach history or work in a museum.

I passed the small reception area, through a set of doors and traipsed down a hallway with rows and rows of cubicles each equipped with a phone headset and computer. A few coworkers stopped there before the official start of the day to chitchat and make slight glances toward me. One supervisor who made his rounds up and down the hallway whistled at me. What a pig. If I reported them, the harassment would increase, or I'd be fired. The caustic part of it all was it didn't begin until word got out Matthew and I had separated.

I ignored him as I entered the locker area, secured my bag in a locker, closed it and took a deep breath. My mind was reeling. Tonight, Joy was spending the night with Matthew and Rebecca. My mom suggested I needed a night to bounce back. She told me to kick back and listen to music. Maybe have a hot bubble bath and prop up my legs and watch movies while drowning my sorrows in wine and ice cream. Then, hopefully, I could get a good night's sleep. Only I wouldn't sleep, as I had to express milk. If I didn't, my supply would dip. Besides, I didn't want *that* woman around my baby either. It all felt so horrible. Breastfeed like a "good" mom or be forced to buy formula I couldn't afford. I knew Matthew would never pay for it either.

My grumpy thoughts were interrupted as I turned to head back down the hallway just as Roger entered.

He stood tall, sporting a new crisp black dress suit. "Hey, Mandy."

I smiled. "Hey." I felt a little insecure, with my wrinkled blouse I hadn't bothered to iron before throwing it on.

He rubbed the back of his neck and sighed. "I hate to be that person. The boss, rather." He winked. Was he trying to be flirty or trying to lighten the mood or both?

I shrugged. "What did I do?" I understood this was a job, and Roger and I, inside these four walls, were merely employees. I was even sure most of the other employees knew we had a thing going on, but the policy was you don't see, hear, or speak of indiscretions. Deny everything, however, it seemed to only apply to the singles for some reason.

"Your numbers are low."

I lightly gnawed my lip. "Oh?" I tensed a bit.

He caressed my upper arm. "Loosen up, Mandy. Go out there and collect some debt."

I nodded. "I will." My inside twisted. I didn't want to suck anyone dry. Alternatively, I was so tired of sticking to that boring script and being yelled at all day by people who didn't want to pay their bills.

Roger looked around the corner from where we stood and then turned to me and planted a kiss on the lips. His gaze was strong. "A little motivation."

I was speechless, my mouth wide open.

"Now get to work," he mumbled. What he wanted was to get laid, and he had no intentions of hiding it, no matter how inappropriate the place.

I turned and approached my work station. It was already a few minutes after eight when I logged on.

I dialed the number to my day's first victim. The phone rang and rang before a click.

"Hello?" I heard a yawn on the other line.

"Can I speak to Rowan Thompson?"

"This is he. Who may I be speaking to?"

I inhaled as quietly as I could. "This is a recorded and monitored line."

I heard heavy breathing. I already knew this wasn't going to be a pleasant call.

"Who are you?" Rowan's voice increased in intensity.

"My name is Amanda. I'm a debt collector with KBD Receivable, Inc. This is an attempt to collect a debt we have on file. Any information obtained will be used for that purpose." I twirled in my chair. I knew what to say by memory—it came second nature.

I heard some grumbling and what resembled an "okay"—a good enough response.

"We have an account in our office with Rowan Thompson totalling a balance of a hundred dollars and thirty-four cents. How would you like to resolve that balance? By phone with a debit or credit card? Or by mail with a check or money order?"

Silence.

"How would you like to resolve this?" I had to keep

myself together and keep on script. My coworkers had repeatedly reminded me that this was business and not to lose control of my emotions, or they'll prey on them. This was especially hard the days following my return to work after Ivory had passed.

"Why don't you give me a second to think about this?" the voice on the other end mumbled.

I sighed. Why couldn't he just tell me he didn't have the money to pay so I could proceed to the next call? I understood fully. In a few short months, I'd be one of these customers. I already had prepared myself to work paycheck to paycheck.

"I'll send in a check in the next few days."

"Okay, I'll let the accounting department know to expect your payment."

He mumbled, "Anything else?"

"Thank you for your time, and we hope you have a great rest of your day."

He hung up without so much as an acknowledgement. So, at least, he was more pleasant than I originally had thought. I took a moment to gather my thoughts before I called the next, and then the next. While every call was a bit different, they were all the same. I hated this job, but with a child to take care of and a divorce pending, I had zero choices.

I picked up the phone and called the next victim. As expected, it ended similarly to the first. I went down the list. Each phone call left me more dead inside. On the last phone call before lunchtime, I was at least able to collect on a $250.00 debt. It was better than nothing. Hopefully enough to keep the boss off my ass.

I dragged myself from the building and sat in my car, locking the door and leaning back. I checked my phone for any messages.

Do you have enough breast milk for the baby? Matthew had texted me.

Yes, there are six bottles. You can drop her off at home tomorrow whenever she has her last bottle. I replied.

Okay.

I stared at the phone, emotions bubbling inside me. My body trembled. I wanted to text him and tell him I was picking Joy up. She had only spent maybe two nights away from me in her short life. But each time, they were with family and not in the same house as Rebecca.

Would you like to go out for supper tonight? Mom's text came across my screen. Her timing couldn't have been better.

Yes, Mom.

I set down the phone and reached into the back seat beside a cooler I used to store breastmilk for my pump. I had just enough time. I lay back staring out the window as I expressed. I longed for the day to be over. Maybe a night away from Joy would be a good thing. I just wished she wasn't around that woman. Maybe I was jealous, but I couldn't help it.

Not even a week after Matthew had moved out, Rebecca had showed her face at my front door to pick up Joy for a visit. She wore a tight-fitting blue satin blouse and a black pencil skirt. Her hair was in a bun without a strand out of place, and she had that stupid smile on her face, where I looked like I had just rolled out of bed, with dark circles under my eyes and dressed in pajama pants with baby puke all over me. It was probably her way of payback for the night at the bar, way back then.

She acted all nice to my face telling me how she'd love Joy like her own. When, in the back of my mind, I wanted to scream. She wasn't Joy's mother. I was. I didn't need her to love my daughter as her own. I needed her to spend as little time around her as possible—no bonding, no pretending to be a second mother. As far as I was concerned, she was a stranger—a convenient hook up for Matthew.

Sudden sadness overcame me. Even though I didn't like Rebecca, I wondered, was this how she had felt when Matthew had broken up with her and gotten with me? Matthew told me they had been together for five years and engaged, but he kept putting it off. It had to rub it in deep for her, as a woman—a victim at the time, I guess—to watch her ex marry another woman after less than a year.

I remembered the text messages between them. One night while he was in the shower, I read a few of them. At least the ones he hadn't deleted. Matthew spent hours in the bathroom texting her. She told him what he was doing was right, because I wasn't there for him. I tried to connect with him. I even begged him to hug me one day when I was crying. He did, but it was forced, out of pity. That was around the time I started flirting with Roger at work on a daily basis. I was still pregnant and not very desirable. After Joy was born and Matthew was spending more time with Rebecca than me, his wife, I gave up, and their affair started full fledged. I sometimes wondered why neither of us had tried harder instead of letting it get to this point. I shook my head, realizing the time.

I finished my pumping session and secured the milk in the cooler. After putting a fresh coat of crimson on my lips, I returned to my cubicle for the second half of the work day. I only needed to keep it together for a few more hours.

I went through the motions. Each phone call was the same script. As much as I hated the job, it helped somewhat. The rest of my life was one big routine.

I ended the last call with five minutes of my shift to spare. A few people hung up, one irate woman screamed every profanity known to mankind at me, but I did get a few to settle their debts. All in all, this was one of my better days.

I twirled in the chair, fiddling with the height-adjustment handle. I just wanted the last minutes to pass so I could bounce out of there.

I couldn't have been happier to end the day. I grabbed my things from the locker and beelined out the door as fast as students on their last day of school. Best of all, there was no work tomorrow.

In the parking lot, I sat debating whether to pump before heading home. I sometimes would pump before picking up Joy. If I waited and she wanted to feed, I didn't get as much. But she wasn't here, and I needed to make up the difference. I said *screw it* and reached back. It wouldn't take that long. After ten minutes and eight ounces, I headed out of the parking lot.

I turned the radio to low and drove. What would I do tonight? After supper with Mom, maybe I'd ask Roger to come over and binge watch reruns of some sappy comedy. I really didn't know.

I tapped my hands to the pop song on the radio. My

mind went blank as I focused on the simple, catchy beat. All of sudden, reality hit me like a ton of bricks. Instead of heading home, I was heading to Joy's daycare. I shook as I saw Matthew's SUV parked in front of the building. Rebecca sat in the passenger seat. My heart sped up as I kept driving.

I no longer wanted the night to myself. I wanted to march back there and retrieve Joy. Dread filled my chest. Matthew and Rebecca would be playing house with my daughter when it should've been Matthew and me enjoying Joy. Not her. Not his girlfriend. I bit my lip. I was jealous. I was never one to be jealous, but venom filled my heart just thinking about her. Why couldn't he have picked anyone but her?

I reached the house as Mom's car was parking out front. I wasted no time getting out of the car as she did the same. I hugged her. My face filled with tears.

She pulled away and wiped a tear from my face. "What's wrong? Bad day at work?"

"Not exactly. I wasn't thinking, drove past the daycare and saw Matthew's car and, well, her." I took a deep breath. "Will it get any easier, Mom?"

Mom patted my shoulder. "I know it's hard, sweetie, but it will."

In the days following him moving out, Mom was my shoulder to cry on. Matthew was lucky he hadn't crossed paths with Mom. She would chew him out. He had promised her he'd be there for me, and he wasn't.

"I really want to go over there and get Joy," I finally admitted.

Mom put her hands on my shoulders. "I know you do.

But Joy is in good hands with her father."

"I don't doubt Matthew isn't taking care of her. I just want her home. She should be home with me. Not with *her*."

Mom shook her head. "Why don't we head out? A distraction is just what you need."

I nodded. Mom was right. There was nothing I could do. This was what divorce was going to look like. It was one of those moments when I wished I had never uttered those words. Matthew would still be home — miserable but home — and not with that woman.

I followed Mom to her car.

"What do you feel like eating?"

I shrugged. "You pick."

"Do you want to go for a walk down by the river?"

I nodded. "Maybe we can stop in the cemetery and visit Ivory?"

Mom sported a concerned expression.

I smiled weakly. "Today was a better day. I didn't think about her as much. I know I'll be sad, but I really want to just say hi."

"Okay," she conceded, still frowning. "I haven't seen my beautiful grandbaby in a while."

Mom pulled away from the curb. I just prayed Matthew didn't show up this time. Every time he was around, it evoked a new wave of emotion. It prevented me from moving on.

Mom parked on a side street, and we exited the car. I strolled beside her in silence for a moment.

"So, have you and Matthew made any leeway on coming to an agreement?" she asked softly.

I sighed. I loved Mom, but why did she bring it up? "No."

"He has a lot of nerve dragging this out."

"It's not him who's dragging it out. It's me."

Mom stopped in the middle of the path. "Why?"

I twirled my hair, avoiding her gaze. "I don't know … I'm not ready, I guess."

Mom didn't say anything as she started walking again. I followed.

"I just haven't come to terms with all that'll change. I'm not ready to put the house on the market nor am I ready to move into a dinky apartment. Matthew, believe it or not, is pushing for me to make an agreement with him. I just want some time to think. I really want to come to terms that my marriage is over." Tears streaked my cheeks.

"I understand, sweetie. But I thought it'd be good for you to move."

"How so?" I already knew what she was going to say.

"With Ivory …" She sported a jaded expression. "You deserve a fresh start. A fresh start is always good. You know, without all those bad memories."

"Let's talk about something else," I snapped. "How about we talk about Dad? How is he?"

"He's good. He's been working long hours out in the fields."

"That's good."

"Next weekend, he'll be home. Maybe you and Joy can stop by for a visit. I'm sure he'd love to see her."

"Okay! Maybe we can spend the night."

Mom beamed.

We finally stopped in front of the cemetery. I had a

change of heart—a sudden realization.

"Second thought, Mom. I'd like to go home. I kind of want to be alone."

My inner strength I thought I'd had vanished. My chest felt heavy. I wanted to go home, crawl under the covers and be alone. I didn't have Joy here with me, and

it'd be simply another reminder of how alone I was.

***

Just before noon the following day, Matthew's SUV pulled up in front of the house. I paced back and forth far enough away from the window in hopes he wouldn't notice from the street how uncomfortable I felt. *She* exited the vehicle. A lump in my throat tightened.

Matthew joined Rebecca on the sidewalk with Joy in one arm and Rebecca holding his other hand. He was still my husband, and she hung on to him as if she was the spouse. She really knew how to rub it in.

I took a deep breath. *Keep it together.* They'll be gone before I know it.

I heard a knock, and, as usual, Matthew opened the door and let himself in. I had considered locking the door just so he'd have to wait for me. Without a second thought, I quickly took Joy from his arms and snuggled her to my chest. She giggled. At least she missed me as much as I did her.

Rebecca stood outside the door, grinning cheek to cheek.

"She did good last night," Matthew said.

"That's good." I faked a smile. Not for him, but more so for Rebecca—to compensate that I was still in my pajamas and my hair was disheveled and to give her the illusion my life was somewhat together.

Rebecca stepped forward. "I never really got a good look inside your house, Matt." I wanted so badly to roll my eyes. She had stepped foot in my entryway multiple times.

"It's nice." That was Matthew's simple response.

She stared at him and smiled. "Maybe someday, we'll move into our own house." She turned to look at me and smiled, her eyes intense. "And I'd make sure Joy had her own space. She is such a doll."

"I know. She is pretty spectacular," I replied and shuffled a bit from toe to toe. "So, it was nice seeing you both, but I'm sure it'll be time for Joy to nurse soon." *Please shut up and leave already.*

Rebecca nudged Matthew's leg with hers, all while maintaining eye contact.

"Oh!" Matthew stammered. "About that. I was hoping to discuss a change in the custody plan."

I stared at Rebecca who didn't move position but just stared.

"You and I can discuss it another time." I kept straight-faced while I burned inside. The sooner *they* both left, the better.

"This week I want to settle everything. No more stalling. Okay?"

"Okeydokey. So, if you don't mind, I have things to do. Have a good afternoon, Matthew." I turned to face Rebecca. "And you as well."

Matthew and Rebecca stepped outside, and I slammed the door behind them. Petty, I realized, but it was better than me exploding on them.

I held Joy to my chest. "I'm so glad you're home with your mommy. Did you have a good time with Dad?"

Joy responded with glee.

I sat on the couch and nursed her. Maybe it was time I contacted a lawyer. I didn't want to keep Matthew from her, because he *was* a good father, but Rebecca rubbed me the wrong way. She must have known I knew what she was doing. She was a fake, manipulative, and not someone who had Joy's best interest at heart. I called it a mother's intuition, and my intuition told me she wasn't to be trusted.

6

I stared at the last text from Matthew. *I've given you an extra week. I don't want to wait anymore. Please, let's talk terms and settle amicably so we can file for divorce. I don't want to drag this out anymore. Please.*

I twirled my hair around my finger while formulating a response. He was right. I was avoiding him. I was also weighing my options and collecting the funds to hire a lawyer. I considered taking some money from the savings account, but then he'd know what I was planning, and I didn't want to tip him off. Not with Rebecca in the wings.

This is what I want. I want primary custody of Joy, no overnights for a year. I want spousal and child support. I want exclusive use of the house for a year, with you covering half the mortgage while I find a way to refinance. I want you to cover half the debt on the car loan and the credit card, and I want half the savings.

I realized I sounded bitter and greedy, when all I wanted was a little bit more time to get some legal advice. I didn't want to be left in the dust. We've been married ten years, and we had built a life together. I wasn't about to let some homewrecker manipulate the situation.

Now, that isn't reasonable.

I half-heartedly chuckled. Of course, he didn't think it was fair. Nothing about this was fair. Losing our daughter and our marriage turning to shit wasn't fair. But it was what it was. He didn't fight for our marriage and wanted us over so badly that he'd have to play hardball.

So, tell me what would be reasonable then?

I rocked back and forth, waiting for his response. Rebecca was likely sitting beside him, telling him what to write—only she underestimated me.

Joy sat in the jumper, bouncing excitedly to her shows. She was my top priority. I couldn't afford to lose her too.

I stood and picked her up. "We're going for a drive. How does that sound?"

She cooed and smiled.

A moment later, I buckled her into the car. "We're going to take a quick drive past Daddy's house, alright?"

The last thing I wanted was to be a stalker. Matthew had reluctantly given me Rebecca's address. I hadn't driven by there yet, but I was entitled to know where my daughter was staying when she wasn't with me.

I put the address in the GPS and headed out. He lived ten minutes away. Half way to their place, my phone blinked from the passenger seat. I ignored it. I would hear what he had to say soon enough.

I reached their street easy enough. I passed rows and rows of condos then her high-rise condo complex. The entrance was locked, and eight-feet-high steel gates surrounded it, so I figured it was secured and assumed she lived in a decent place. I had half hoped he had moved into some dump.

I sighed as I drove home, when a few more notifications caught my attention. Probably Matthew in a frenzy. I glanced in the rear view. The mirror attached to the back seat showed me Joy sleeping.

I pulled into a nearby store parking lot and snatched my phone.

I want one overnight a week. I want to sell the house. I don't want to pay for a house I'm not living in. The car, you pay for. It's yours. As for the credit card, I'll pay the charges I made to it. I'll continue to support Joy. But remember, divorce means we go our separate ways.

I took a deep breath as I replied. *We're married, and half the debt is your problem whether you like it or not. As for the house, you left me to scramble, so I deserve more time. My original offer stands.*

I clenched my fists as I waited for his answer to come through.

That's unreasonable. He replied.

I guess we have a problem, don't we?

I closed his message to see another text from an unknown number. I opened it.

Hello. This is Rebecca. I know you probably don't want to hear from me, but I just wanted to message you and talk woman to woman. I know this isn't any of my business, but I know you're dealing with a lot, and please know Matthew is as well. Please don't drag this out any longer. Please settle with him so we can all move on with our lives. Joy deserves two parents who are happy, so don't drag her into the middle of this.

I stared into the rear-view mirror at Joy and back at the phone. My jaw clenched. The nerve of the bitch. I began to text a huge rant when I stopped myself. After taking a few deep breaths, I simply responded: *You're right. This isn't any of your business. Matthew and I will handle this. Thanks.*

My body shook. Tears burned my eyes. I took a deep breath.

I want to talk to a lawyer, I texted Matthew. *I want this to be amicable, but I don't feel comfortable discussing this further without legal advice. I have you on one end and your girlfriend on the other pressuring me. I just want to look out for my and Joy's best interests. I hope you understand.*

I needed to keep this business. This was a business transaction. I had to keep my emotions out of it, as hard as it would be. Rebecca and Matthew were together, a unit, and I was the obstacle. So, if I treated this as business, they couldn't catch me off guard.

I'm sorry she messaged you. She's just concerned. Please let's talk about it. I'll pay off the car loan if you cover the credit card bill.

I took a deep breath. *What's the rush? It just feels like you're trying to pull a fast one on me. And Rebecca isn't "concerned." She's trying to cause drama.*

I swore at myself. I needed to remember to keep this business. Matthew wasn't on my side. He didn't want me. I doubt if he even loved me anymore, otherwise, he wouldn't be doing this to me.

She's just nervous. You remember how we met. She was really hurt. I don't want to ruin a good thing.

I rolled my eyes and switched from his name to text Roger.

Hey, handsome! I finished the text with an emoticon. Lately, I've been trying to distance myself from Roger, but every time I tried to, I pulled myself back in. I wanted to feel something. The hurt was there. I didn't care how Rebecca felt. I thought I could relate to her, but she was a homewrecker. It wasn't my fault back then that Matthew wanted me.

Well, hello, Mandy. How are you? It's been a while.

The flutters in my heart intensified. *I'm just grabbing*

something to eat.

I wasn't sure what I was hoping to gain from this encounter. I hoped he would at least entertain a conversation, even for a little bit so I didn't view myself as just a means of sexual pleasure.

I switched to my conversation with Matthew and read his next text.

I just want to keep this affordable for the both of us.

I sighed. *Tell you what. Have Rebecca stay out of it and I won't hire a lawyer. Deal?*

I returned to my conversation with Roger.

I can't talk right now. But maybe tomorrow before work, we can fit in a quickie.

I didn't respond. I sat in the car dejectedly.

Are you home? Matthew texted.

I was heading home from the store. I lied.

I'm going to stop by. Maybe if we are face to face, in private, it'll be easier.

Okay, fine. I'll head home now.

If he didn't bring Rebecca, I could stand to be around him.

See ya in an hour, so no rush.

I drove home. Carefully taking Joy out of the car seat, despite my best efforts, she woke up. Inside the house, I plopped her in the bouncer. She wasn't fussy, and I needed a few to get myself together.

I headed to the bathroom. I stared at my reflection in the mirror. Have I ever let myself go? No wonder Matthew didn't desire me anymore. I looked like shit—all flabby from giving birth. I never dressed up anymore, and I never looked put together.

I turned on the shower, stripping my clothes and letting myself soak under the stream. Afterward, with only a towel wrapped around my waist, I headed for the bedroom. I rummaged through my dresser for something to wear. Something spectacular. Something sexy. I wanted to know if he still found me attractive instead of just the mother of his child and his soon-to-be ex-wife.

In the corner of my bottom drawer, I found a pair of black jeans. My hand trembled as I retrieved them. *Here's hoping these fit.* I hadn't worn them since before I found out I was pregnant with Joy, maybe even on the day I got the positive pregnancy test.

I managed to pull them over my butt and fastened them. They felt a bit tight. Well, really tight, but they fit. Matthew always said I looked good in them every time I wore them. Even Ivory … I paused. She would copy her dad and said I looked good in them. Seemed cute and silly back then, but now I'd do anything to hear those words.

I grabbed a clean short-sleeve V-neck sweater. As I expected, it showed a bit of cleavage and covered my flab. I did a three sixty spin and smiled. I didn't look half bad, and I didn't look like I was heading for the club.

I quickly combed my hair and applied a bit of makeup. I didn't want it to appear obvious I was trying to get him to notice me. I half expected him not to even care, especially if the last year was any indication of how screwed up our marriage had become.

In the living room, I waited for him to arrive. I prayed he kept his promise to not include Rebecca. I paced. I always paced these days. Nothing surprised me anymore, but I hoped he could give me this one little thing.

A few minutes later, he showed. He did his usual ritual—knocked and let himself in. It felt different, him knocking, when it was just him, especially when he wasn't picking up Joy. It almost felt like we were back to the way things were before I asked for a divorce.

"Hey."

I stood there leaning against the doorframe, my hip sticking out. "Hello." It shouldn't be this uncomfortable being around the man I spent over ten years of my life with. Why was this so weird?

Matthew took off his jacket and lay it over the bench by the door before entering the living room. He approached Joy and kneeled to her level. "Hey, baby girl."

Joy cooed.

He gently kissed her forehead and rose. He went to sit on the couch, and I did the same.

"Well?" I asked.

Matthew brushed the back of his neck and exhaled. "It's just been awhile. Almost seems like I am a stranger, you know?"

I nodded. "Yeah." I wound my hair around my finger, my knuckle turning white before releasing. "I know what you mean. Nothing's the same anymore."

Matthew darted his gaze toward me. "I know it's hard right now, Amanda. Neither of us wanted to get to this point. But once it's over, it'll get easier."

I turned away and mumbled, "It would've been easier if you were here for me when I needed you."

"What?"

"Nothing."

Matthew frowned. "Don't lie to me. What did you

say?"

My face grew hot as I placed my hand on my constricting chest. "It doesn't matter. It won't change anything anyway." I sighed as tears welled in my eyes.

"Don't cry." He looked away. "Don't do this."

I gnawed my upper lip. "Out of everyone, you had to choose her. You must love rubbing her in my face every chance you get." Why was I bringing this up? Why was I torturing myself like this?

"And yet you keep bringing your boss into my house."

I stood, my body tensing. "Instead of being there for me, you started hooking up with your ex. Instead of coming home to grieve with me, you were staying at work, texting her. What did you expect me to do?" I took a deep breath, fury consuming me. "Did you expect me to stay put? Crying for you to be there for me? No. I wanted to feel wanted too. Because you weren't there. You weren't there!" I yelled then turned and patrolled. We kept having this same conversation repeatedly. But this time, I just felt defeated. "It made me wonder if you ever really, truly loved me."

I wasn't sure if my comment was directed at him or to myself. My self-confidence was shot.

"I do. I did love you."

"Funny way of showing it."

"I didn't come over here to hash this out with you."

I stopped and stared. "Yeah, I know." I paused. "You came here to tell me you want to sell the damn house so you can eliminate any traces of our once happy life. You want to forget about me, about Joy, and about Ivory. But do you know what, Matthew? Hmm. You can't replace what we had. You can't just walk out this door and pretend like Ivory didn't die!"

"Why are you bringing up Ivory?" His voice was filled with dismay.

"Because everything comes back to her. If only you were watching her, she'd still be here. My baby would still be here."

I lowered my head and swallowed hard. Why did I keep bringing it up? Nothing we could do would bring her back. Throwing it in his face wouldn't change anything. I gripped my shirt and clenched my jaw. I was so angry, so bitter. I realized just how much hurt I felt. My heart bled. I wanted to feel whole again, but it wasn't possible.

"You never told me you went inside," Matthew shot back then looked away.

I didn't respond.

"I'm sorry. Okay, Amanda? I'm sorry things turned out this way, but I can't change things. I can't change what happened. And I can't change that I fell in love with Rebecca again. I never intended to fall for her again, but I did. I'm just trying to move on, like you."

I didn't respond. My heart was shattered. I knew he had fallen for Rebecca again, but to hear him say those words pierced me deep. How could he just fall out of love for me just like that? We fell for each other so hard. We were so in love. We did everything together—the nights we had, the road trips, and holidays. We had it all. The perfect life. The perfect family. Now, we had nothing left.

"You'll find happiness again. You'll find love."

I didn't make eye contact with him. "I want some more time before selling." I kept my voice low. "I still need to go through Ivory's old things. We need to divide up our stuff. I'll start by claiming all the antiques."

"Okay. Can I have the big screen TV?"

"Once I get myself another TV."

"Fair enough."

"Do you want any of the photographs of the kids?"

Matthew approached me and put his hand on my shoulder. "I will always care about you."

I jerked him away. "Do you want any of the photographs of the kids?"

"Yes."

For the next while, we both discussed what we each wanted from the house. I avoided looking at him. I needed to get this over with. I would let him go. I'd let him be with Rebecca. Maybe she was always the love of his life.

"See, that wasn't so hard," Matthew said.

"How about we meet up again in a few days to talk some more? I really need to make supper and get Joy ready for bed."

"Alright. We made good progress though."

He tried to hug me, but I pulled away. "Have a good night, Matthew."

He grimaced. "Goodnight."

Once he left, I crumpled to the floor, tears streaming down my face. Joy began to cry in the background. I tried to move for her, but I couldn't. My heart was shattered.

From What's Broken

Part Two
Matthew

7

Rebecca nudged me, but I pretended to be asleep. She shook me again. I groaned but didn't move. She heaved out a single weighty breath. It felt like someone was sitting on my chest. Why did I promise her that we'd visit her parents this afternoon? I wasn't ready to tell them that we were back together. They loved me when we first dated, but then I broke her heart. There was no way they'd give me another chance, was there?

The entirety of the quaint, little town we both came from talked about how much they hated me. What would they think about Rebecca giving me another chance? The neighbors and all our close friends would have something to say. Her folks came from a conservative community, and I knew all too well how much they frowned upon married men dating before getting divorced. They had spread rumors that Amanda was my mistress back in the day, but that hadn't been the case. It was true I had moved on, but I hadn't cheated on Rebecca. Not like I had done to Amanda.

She nudged me harder. "Come on, Matt. Wake up."

I grumbled and turned over to make eye contact with her. "I'm getting up. I didn't sleep well last night." It was the truth. I slept maybe a few hours max and not all at once. I don't remember the last time I slept well. I tried not to bog her down with all those extra details. Maybe when my divorce was finalized, I'd be more open with her. Right now, my main goal was to avoid pissing off Amanda too much. She could make my life a living hell in this custody battle, especially since I didn't know why she was being so mean.

She rose and smiled. "I'll make a pot of coffee. So, get your ass in gear."

I smiled back. "Thanks." Sitting up on the bed and forcing my legs over the side, I reached for my phone, yawned, and checked for any messages—just a few from work and one from Mom. I texted her back a simple *Good morning*. The work ones could wait until later tonight. It was my day off. I stood up, wearing just my boxers, and approached the kitchen. A shot of caffeine and maybe even a shot or two of vodka would loosen me up before we left.

Rebecca stood over the kitchen sink, staring out the window at the pool below. "Those little brats are at it again," she mumbled.

I walked up beside her and peered out the window to see what all her fuss was about. I shrugged as I grabbed myself a cup of coffee. "They're kids. Kids splash and horseplay. It's what they do." I wanted to roll my eyes but didn't want to offend her. Over time, as Joy grew older, she'd realize kids made messes and got into mischief. She's already warmed up to stinky diapers. Well, at least she no longer acted like they're a big deal.

"I guess." She almost threw my favorite mug at me. "Hurry. Have your coffee so we can hit the road."

I glanced above the stove. It was only a quarter after nine. I wouldn't say it, but I missed sleeping late on weekends. Rebecca liked to be up, have eaten breakfast and have finished grocery shopping all before noon, while all I wanted was to sleep until eleven and relax after working all week. Well, except when I had Joy, but that was different.

I glanced at the liquor cabinet above the stove. "Dear? Could you find me something to wear? You know, to visit your parents and all. You'll know better than me." In reality, I just wanted to distract her so I could get my hands on some vodka.

She obliged, and I quickly got up, grabbed a bottle and took a shot. I was about to replace the bottle but decided on a second. I rinsed the shot glass and returned it to its spot. Sitting down, I quickly downed the rest of my coffee then sauntered to the bathroom. I needed to get rid of the booze breath. The last time I didn't, she found out and was pissed for days. I didn't want to give them another reason to hate me.

Rebecca entered the bathroom and set a change of clothes onto the toilet seat. She wrapped her arms around my waist. "Don't worry, hun. Today will go well. Maybe you can see if Joy can come. Who doesn't like babies?"

I shook my head. "I don't think Amanda will go for that."

Rebecca shrugged. "Don't tell her you're bringing her to visit my parents. You know you don't owe her any explanations."

Well, Amanda did bring her lover around my daughter and inside my house, so I didn't think there would be any problem with Joy meeting Rebecca's parents. That was, if Amanda allowed me to take her. Ever since I moved out, she had become more overprotective, which was understandable, I assumed. She had turned into someone I barely knew. Whatever—soon it'd all be over. We'll be divorced and I won't have to walk on eggshells around her anymore. It was all so sad. I had loved her, and we used to get along so well. I really don't know where it all went wrong. But it would get better, wouldn't it?

"Well, are you going to call her?" Rebecca asked.

I reluctantly refocused to the present, nodded, and dialed Amanda. I paced back and forth, hoping she would cooperate. If she weren't breastfeeding our daughter, I would never have agreed to let her have this much control over when and how often I spent time with my daughter. Just a few more months and Amanda can wean her early, and we won't need to tolerate this anymore.

"Hello?" Amanda mumbled with exasperation.

She's in one of her moods. I just know it.

"What do you want?" she demanded before I could respond. Why did she always do that? I got that she was pissed at me and at everything. But what could I do to change that?

I rubbed the back of my neck. "I want to see Joy for the day." I glanced at Rebecca.

Her hands rested on her hips, and she glared at me. "Tell her it's your day."

I waved her away.

"You know that today is *my* day with her," Amanda snapped.

I sighed. "I just miss her. What's wrong with me spending part of the day with her? You can catch up on sleep or do whatever you want." I paused. "It'll just be her and me," I lied. Why did it bother me so much to lie to her?

"How long were you thinking?"

I mouthed to Rebecca, *How long?*

She held up a five.

"Around supper time."

Rebecca shook her head in disbelief. I guess I didn't quite get the memo. What was with women not being crystal clear? It annoyed the hell out of me back when we last dated too.

"Fine!"

"I'll be over to pick her up right away."

Amanda mumbled something else before hanging up. She was pissed, and she would be even more pissed if I told her about my true intentions. I loved Joy, but I needed to make a good impression and keep my promise to Rebecca. How could I prove to her that I was committed? She had her apprehensions and for good reason. I dumped her once. I couldn't face her folks without making it clear that I would never hurt their daughter again.

I turned to her. "Okay, she has no problem with me taking Joy for the day."

Rebecca rolled her eyes and looked unimpressed. "Why do you feel the need to ask for permission?"

I held up my hand at her. "Shoot, Rebecca. What do you want from me? I want to keep the peace."

"You're her father. You deserve to see her more than a few hours at a time." She looked away and mumbled, "I sometimes doubt her ability to take care of an infant."

I didn't respond. I should have, because Amanda was a great mother. But I had a duty to be there for my girlfriend.

"Ready to go, love?"

Rebecca smiled and nodded.

The drive to the house was quiet. Would Amanda yell at me? Would she play twenty questions because she had nothing better to do?

As we approached the block, I turned to glance at Rebecca. "I'm going to park a few houses down. I don't want Amanda to see you. I don't want any drama. I just want today to go well."

Rebecca sighed and opened her mouth to object.

"I'm just nervous about meeting your parents after so many years, all right? Can we discuss this another time?"

"Okay. Pull over, and I'll wait until you come around to pick me up."

I grinned as I pulled in front of the park a half block from my home. *My old home,* I sadly reminded myself. Pretty soon, a realtor would be staking a For Sale sign into the front lawn, finally ending that sham. The weight on my shoulders intensified. Everything was happening so fast. Were we making the right decision?

I couldn't think about that now. I parked, headed to the front door, and waited. I took a deep breath and turned the doorknob, but it was locked. I don't have the key anymore. Why didn't I take a spare with me?

I rang the doorbell, annoyed. I was locked out of my own house.

Amanda opened the door holding Joy. She frowned, sporting her usual frumpy look. Her hair was in a half-assed bun, and dark circles outlined her eyes. When we had been together, she would never even step out to get the mail without at least brushing her hair. Now she didn't have a care in the world. She had really let herself go. She wasn't the woman I had married, that was for sure. I wanted to say something but kept my mouth shut.

"Hello," I mumbled.

Amanda glanced into Joy's eyes. "You have a good day

with your dad."

I stood there waiting for her to hand over Joy, but she didn't. She sighed dejectedly, her shoulders slumped, and a blank stare looked back at me.

"What's wrong?" I asked, rubbing the back of my neck. It was a lose-lose situation. If I didn't ask, she'd react negatively. Her bold personality was what had attracted me to her in the first place, but, right now, it seemed like a curse.

Her face sagged, and her mouth upturned as she asked, "Why do you care?"

I gulped. "Well ..." How do I respond to this without hurting her feelings? She was way too sensitive these days. Besides, this wasn't appropriate. Rebecca wouldn't like this, and she was waiting.

"Well, what?"

I clenched my jaw and gritted my teeth. "I hope you have a better day, Amanda. I really should get going. I'll have Joy back this evening."

Amanda wiped away a partly formed tear as she handed Joy to me. She turned to grab a diaper bag nearby. "There should be enough breast milk until after supper."

"Thanks."

Joy babbled happily as we walked to the car. From around a corner, a car screeched past. My heart raced, stopping me in my tracks. I saw her lifeless body lay in the street for a moment. Would I ever forget that day?

I shook my head and buckled Joy into the car seat. I really needed to get out of here. Maybe slip another shot before we reach their house. But I had already taken two shots within the last hour and didn't want to risk being drunk. Why couldn't I just ask Rebecca to postpone this meeting until after my divorce was finalized?

I drove to the block where Rebecca waited.

"Took you long enough."

"Sorry."

She frowned.

Before pulling away, I brushed some of the hair from her face and glanced into her striking eyes.

The tightness in her face loosened.

"There, that's better," I said, appeasing her.

"They're expecting us. We should go."

I nodded. *Here's goes nothing.*

When we arrived, Rebecca's mother greeted us. They lived in the very same brick ranch house as when Rebecca and I had dated long ago. Her mother still looked the same, intimidating as ever. I could have sworn countless eyes glared all over me—the piece of shit who broke Rebecca's heart. I glanced in the mirror to see Joy attached to the back seat. Amanda was always attentive when it came to car seat safety, even more so after Joy was born.

Joy played with her feet. At least she was here to make this day more manageable. She stared at me. I quickly exited the car and went to the other side to grab Joy.

"Well, hello, Matthew. I didn't expect to see you." She looked at Joy. "And I see you brought a little cutie."

"I-it's nice to see you, Marge. I-I mean Mrs. Larsen. And yes, thanks. This is my daughter, Joy."

She wrinkled her nose but managed a weak smile. "I'm so glad you and Rebecca have found your way back to one another."

Rebecca shuffled from foot to foot. "Mom, we're living

together."

Marge stroked her neck. "Why don't we go inside and talk."

Rebecca shot me a look as she followed her mother. I quickly grabbed the diaper bag and followed. Brock, Rebecca's father, stood at the top of the stairs.

"Rebecca brought Matthew with her. Isn't that great?" Marge said. Her voice was monotone, not a hint of excitement.

Brock stared at me. "Who's the baby?"

"This is my daughter, Joy."

Brock took several steps toward me.

"Why don't you let me hold her, Matt?" Rebecca asked.

I reluctantly handed Joy to her.

Brock outstretched his hand, and we shook. His grip was strong and his glare intense. "Now, shall we go and enjoy the meal Marge prepared?"

"Yes. Thanks for having Joy and me in your home, Mr. Larsen." I rolled back my shoulders.

At the kitchen table, we said grace and passed around food while I held Joy.

"Rebecca," Marge said. "Why don't you run into the basement and get that old highchair so the baby has somewhere to sit?"

As Rebecca left the table, Marge and Brock made small talk, not saying a single word to me or even acknowledging me. It was a blessing, but it also meant they didn't want me here. The feeling was mutual. I nervously bounced Joy on my knee.

Rebecca returned to the table with an old highchair. I opened my mouth to say I couldn't use that. Amanda's concerned voice echoed in my head. But this was a battle not worth fighting. "Thanks." I carefully placed Joy in the old highchair and strapped her in with the fraying straps. I'd never hear the end of it if Joy got hurt.

After eating in silence for a few moments, Marge spoke. "So, how long have you been divorced?"

I gulped, almost choking on my food. "I'm actually not divorced yet. We're separated, and my wife and I are discussing how to divide up our assets."

Brock sipped the wine from the glass sitting in front of him. "That's what lawyers are for, something a corporate person like yourself should know."

I nodded. "I just want to keep things amicable — for Joy."

"So, Joy is an only child?" Marge chimed in.

I took a deep breath. Why couldn't they just change the subject? But I promised Rebecca to be honest and polite. "Not exactly." I glanced away.

Rebecca lifted her plate. "Mom, can you pass the potatoes?"

She passed the potatoes.

"So, do you have other children with your wife?" Brock asked. "Or … with anyone else? I just want to know who's going to be in your life."

"I had a daughter, Ivory." I put down my fork and twisted my lips.

"Oh? And why couldn't she make it tonight?"

Rebecca rubbed my thigh and mouthed, *Sorry*.

I glanced downward. "She died." My legs clenched. "She died," I repeated. The bottle of red wine in the center of the table called my name. The first few weeks after her funeral I spent many nights drinking at the bar. It was getting better, but I still didn't want to talk about it. Not with them.

"I'm so sorry," Marge said with a bit of genuine sadness. At least it was a step in the right direction.

"Why don't we talk about something else?" Rebecca suggested.

Brock, who hadn't even attempted to hide his disdain for me, crossed his arms and leaned back in his chair. "So, how'd she die?"

"She got hit by a car." I stood up. "If you'll excuse me." I turned to Rebecca. "Keep an eye on Joy. I just need a few minutes."

I walked out the front door and slumped on the step. After a moment, I slipped through the front door. In the hallway, I overheard Brock talking to Rebecca.

"It's so convenient, isn't it? That he's back with you after his kid died?"

"It's not like that, Dad."

"This isn't one of your better choices. But, what can I say? You haven't brought home a decent one yet."

Ouch!

I bit my lip. It was true. If Ivory hadn't died, Amanda and I would still be together. But it happened. Ivory died and so did my marriage. Amanda and I didn't love each other anymore. At least, not like we used to. I still cared for her, but it wasn't love. I returned to the kitchen and reluctantly sat at the table.

Brock poured himself another glass of wine.

"May I?" I asked.

"Of course," Marge said.

I poured myself a glass, chugged the wine a little quickly, and carefully set the glass on the table. "I know you two aren't thrilled we're back together, but I can promise this time is for real, and I can promise I won't hurt her again."

Deep down I didn't care what they thought of me. Rebecca and I hadn't been getting along back then. I didn't necessarily regret breaking up and getting with Amanda, but I needed to swallow my pride, because I didn't want them hating me forever.

Brock clenched his jaw. "Let's hope so. If not, we'll have a problem, won't we?"

"It'll be different this time."

Brock twirled his glass, staring at the contents and taking a swig before changing the subject

8

My hand hovered above her cheek, and I brushed the side of Rebecca's face then kissed her. She pulled away, an intense gaze fixated on me, but she smiled, crooked and amiss. She touched my lips with one finger when I reached in for another kiss. She skimmed her fingertips along my jawline a little too rough for my comfort. Then she plopped backward on the bed with a slight grimace adorning her face.

"What's wrong?" I asked.

She pinched her lips together while gripping the sheets, her knuckles turning white, and glared.

I swallowed hard. "What's wrong, baby?" I asked again. Why was she mad? What had I done this time? No matter what I did these days, I was always pissing off someone, whether it was Amanda or Rebecca. I just couldn't win. I was confused though. Last night, Rebecca and I had a good night. We were having a good morning, at least before she returned from the kitchen.

"My mom called" — she paused and took a long, drawn breath — "after not returning my calls all week. Can you believe it?"

I gritted my teeth. I knew after meeting them, they hated me, and I hadn't made a good impression. Did they not like Joy? They barely acknowledged her or talked to her. Everybody talked to Joy. Maybe they were too busy thinking about how I drank one too many glasses of wine. I had two — or maybe it was three glasses. I couldn't really remember, because I was so tense, and Rebecca ended up driving us home. I was feeling a bit of a warm rush. I couldn't help it. I squeezed my fist, thinking about Ivory. After talking about her, everything had gone to hell.

When she didn't answer, I prodded. "So? What did she have to say, babe?"

"I-I got a lecture." Her jaw clenched, and her face deepened to a cherry red. "They think you're not serious. They think I'm making a huge mistake."

I stood up and glared at her. "You know I'm serious, don't ya?" I didn't know what else I could do to show her I was here for her—that she was my choice, not Amanda.

She didn't make eye contact and just hugged her legs to her chest. "It was a lot of little things."

"Such as?" I plopped beside her just as she moved to sit beside me.

"They aren't impressed that you're still married."

"We already kind of knew they wouldn't be happy about that." I sighed. I had tried to warn her, but she kept insisting.

She stared at me, her body tightened, and her fist clenched. "My dad smelled alcohol on your breath before dinner. Were you drinking before we went over there?"

I shook my head without even thinking. "It was from the night before. Or in the middle of the night. I couldn't sleep. I'm sorry." I tried to keep a straight face. Why was I lying to her? If she found out I lied, all hell would break loose. It'd show her I couldn't be trusted, and she'd be crushed—so hurt after she was there for me. But the truth was I didn't want to get scolded. I didn't want to keep making excuses or to have to explain to her I used alcohol as a crutch, and it was how I coped.

"Then at dinner, you were drinking. *A lot.* I counted four glasses."

Oh shit, I thought. I waited for her to continue. If my time with Amanda had taught me anything, it was women needed to be listened to. I wish I had done more of it.

"I know it was because Ivory got brought up. I'm sorry. I really am ..." She shifted in her seat.

I sat eagerly. "You told them it's been hard on me?" Maybe, just maybe, if they understood — even if just her mother understood, being a mother and all — it would make this better. Women were always more compassionate when it came to grieving or more likely to be empathic, or something. Having them not on my side wasn't a good thing.

Rebecca nibbled her upper lip. "No, I didn't." She looked away. "You didn't make a good impression. Nothing I could say would've made a difference. If anything, it'd piss them off more." She stood again and paced. "You're making this hard. I want to be there for you. I want to be the support your wife wasn't when you needed her. But I'm hurting too. I'm confused, and I'm anxious you'll go back to her. My parents are too." She stopped and stared at me. "My dad is furious we're living together, not married, while you're still married to another woman. And not to mention that you have a kid. He's not thrilled about that."

I sighed. "I know."

"What do you mean you *know*? Did my dad say something to you?"

I took a deep breath. "I overheard your dad telling you how convenient it was that, after my daughter died, we hooked up." He had made it almost sound like I wanted my daughter to die, that I planned for it to happen that way. The very thought made me so irate my vision shilly-shallied.

Rebecca twisted her mouth. She was blasé. "So, you're eavesdropping on my private conversations now?"

I couldn't listen to this anymore, and her being insensible to my anger made me even more upset. "No, I wasn't listening in. I walked in to them talking shit that isn't true. I'm sorry your folks hate me" — I slid on a pair of boxers — "but I won't sit here and defend what was out of my control. I didn't plan any of this. My daughter died, my marriage went to shit, and you and I reconnected. That is all there is to it. They can either accept it or they don't. What really matters is what are *you* going to do about it?" There. I let it out and put the ball in her court. I couldn't change it. Oh well, she was a big girl. Either she wanted to be with me or would let her parents control her, like they had before. They'd had way too much input in our relationship back then.

I grabbed a shirt from the closet and slipped it over my head. Without a second glance, I left for the kitchen. What was I doing? Why was I so angry at Rebecca? At her parents? I knew they had every reason to not trust me. I did dump Rebecca after all. I did end our engagement a few months before our wedding and marry another woman.

I poured myself a glass of water. Staring at the cup, I contemplated making a shot of vodka and soda, but I stopped myself. Drinking wouldn't solve my problems. It'd only make things worse — it'd make the tension even worse.

Was it worth it? No, I told myself. It wasn't.

Rebecca ambled into the kitchen and didn't say a word, wearing one of my baggy nightshirts. I believe Amanda wore it at one point, too, but I wouldn't dare tell Rebecca that. Why was I even thinking about my wife when this dazzling figure stood before me? I shook my head, trying to clear it, but it was no use.

The revelation of the day I had met Amanda filled my head. Rebecca and I weren't doing well. She was knee-deep in wedding preparations, and I was overwhelmed. We argued constantly. She had shut me out, not letting me make any decisions for what was supposed to be our special day. She told me it wasn't normal that, as a man, I would want any input in flowers or the whole nine yards. She demanded the best, but instead of causing more arguing and more stress, I let her handle everything. I silenced any suggestion, any idea I may have had. She knew I had a high standard, too, as Amanda would say when we first met.

Oh, how I fell hard for Amanda that night in the bar. She wore that tight red dress, and she was cute, flirty, and mesmerising. I knew Rebecca was jealous, but I was too selfish, too self-centered to care. I told Amanda all about my relationship problems, and she understood me like Rebecca never did.

Rebecca shuffled past me to the fridge. She pulled it open and yanked out the milk. The bowl and spoon clattered on the counter. I jumped. It struck me. I did the same thing to Rebecca way back then—ran from my problems into the arms of my wife. Now I was back with the woman I had left in the first place.

Here I was with a second chance with my first real love. Only I was older, and I could handle her now, where I had been too blind and immature before. I had to make it up to her. She deserved that much.

I lowered my shoulders. "Don't be mad."

"I'm not," she said, not looking at me.

But she was. Her tone told me all, not to mention the mess she was making. Milk was everywhere. She didn't seem to care she was making a mess. Amanda would have cleaned it up, but no, Rebecca acted like it wasn't there.

I kept my mouth shut. That's what good boyfriends do after all. They didn't criticize and certainty didn't compare their partners to their ex.

She finally turned to me. "Look, you really need to get this divorce finalized. Stop stalling and hire a lawyer. I really don't care, but, once it's final, my parents will know you're serious. They'll back off. I know they will. They used to love you, remember?"

I did remember. I remember the day I sat with Mr. Larsen and asked for his blessing in marrying Rebecca. I had been nervous. I had cut myself in three different places while shaving that morning, because I had been a wreck. A man, afraid? It was embarrassing, but Rebecca was pressuring me to propose for months, so I took the plunge. He and I had enjoyed a beer, and I had asked him. Without a second thought, he nodded and welcomed me into his family. I had known them for almost five years at that point. It was just a formality, since I was basically like a son to them anyway.

I not only threw it back in his face, but a few months after we broke up, I ran into him. I didn't even say hello or apologize. They had paid the deposit on the hall and had paid for Rebecca's wedding dress. I showed Brock just how egocentric and ungrateful I was when I walked right on by, smug as ever. I kept telling myself I didn't owe him anything.

Now, here I was, trying to win them back. I wished they'd accept me. Rebecca's family was her backbone, and I was just the piece of shit, not-yet-divorced husband with a child who was hooking up with their daughter. It was not a good feeling.

"Well, are you going to get it done?" Rebecca paced, her cereal forgotten for now. "Besides, it was her who wanted the divorce in the first place, yet she's dragging her feet. She's playing you, Matthew! She wants to play the victim, when she's the one who pulled the plug. I don't get it."

I opened my mouth to speak, but she interrupted me yet again.

"And don't bother telling me it's complicated. I get it. She's depressed. She's sad. Well, you are too. It's not your job to pick her up when she falls. She needs to accept that you moved on." Rebecca gulped. "I hate to bring her up, but it's not healthy for Joy to be around such negativity. I do sometimes worry about Amanda's mental health. Not to say she'd do anything ..."

I couldn't stand another minute of this craziness. To shut her up, I planted a kiss on Rebecca's forehead. Amanda wasn't crazy. Not her. She was too strong, even in her grief, to be a risk to Joy. She was angry, jealous, and wanted to make it known. That's all it was. But I had to keep the peace, and I needed to hurry and get this over with. Maybe I'd just agree to let Amanda stay in the house for a year, like she wanted. She wouldn't be able to refinance unless she found a better job anyway, and I'd still get half the equity. Rebecca didn't know about the savings, so maybe I could just offer her all the money, and she'd pay the debts with what would be my half.

"I'm going to tell her today my final offer, and if she doesn't accept it, I'll contact a lawyer. Okay?"

"Okay!"

I wanted to sigh but didn't. Instead, I swallowed hard and ate my words for breakfast. I appeased Rebecca, for now, at least. But I wasn't sure I could stand up to Amanda. I didn't want to involve a lawyer. I didn't want to eat up what little equity we had. Most of all, I didn't want to hurt Amanda more than she was already feeling. But I couldn't tell Rebecca that. There was a lot I couldn't tell Rebecca.

She stared at me with a concerned expression on her face. She had to sense my uncertainty, so I reached in and kissed her. Kissing her always worked, if only temporarily to avoid having to talk about how I really felt. I had to figure out a way to convince Amanda to agree to my offer.

9

Rebecca hovered over me as I texted Amanda. *We need to talk.* I set the phone down and turned my attention to Rebecca. She played with the necklace around her neck,bouncing from foot to foot and biting her upper lip. She stared at me, always wanting to know what I was saying to Amanda. She wanted this divorce over so badly, and I couldn't wait to give it to her. I wanted to make Rebecca happy, at least so she would leave me alone.

"Now that wasn't so hard, was it, babe?" she insisted, her voice almost a whine.

"No, no it wasn't," I admitted, but it was hard, and it was about to get a lot worse. Amanda was going to flip, and I could only imagine the world of pain I was going to walk into. I knew her all too well. She was going to fight me. She already hated Rebecca, and she'd hate her that much more if I went back on my word. Why couldn't they get along? Why must I be in the middle?

Okay, whatever. I have a box of stuff for you to pick up anyway. We can talk then. Just leave her at home.

When Rebecca huffed, beads of perspiration formed on my forehead. I knew she didn't trust Amanda and didn't want us alone for any amount of time, but she needed to be patient, for just a bit longer. Then, we could really jumpstart our future, just how she wanted. Everything we discussed, our hopes and dreams, would finally come true—or mostly hers, at least, but I needed a clean break first. She just didn't understand it, but that was fine.

"You aren't going to entertain this? Why can't you just tell her, right now, through text, that you are done *negotiating*. It's always an excuse for you." She looked downward, her face contoured as if she'd cry. "You still want her don't you? Or what are you so afraid of? I'm so sick of being treated likes shit."

I shook my head frantically as I tried to reach for her hand. "No, hun."

She pushed me away. "Then why can't you do this one thing for me?"

I heaved a sigh. "I just don't want a big huge legal battle. It will be expensive, and you don't know Amanda like I do." I paused, trying to choose my words carefully. "She can be, well, bitter. I'd love to come out of my divorce with some money left. I promised you I wouldn't drag this out. I know she will react badly, and any progress we've made will be lost. Trust me. It's better to get her to believe she's getting a fair deal, than to have her fight me and we both end up with nothing."

Rebecca rolled her eyes. "Fine. But today, you promised me you'd get a lawyer if she didn't agree."

I turned away from her to send my text with privacy. *I'll come by later,* I responded. How was I going to pull this off? Working all day, doing hours and hours of paperwork and negotiating with a top executive wasn't this stressful.

Do you know what? I'll just drop this stuff off. And I'll have my final offer ready. That was Amanda's response. I stared at Rebecca and relayed what Amanda texted. Rebecca just shrugged sporting a little grin.

I wonder if Rebecca had messaged her again. She promised me she wouldn't, but I wouldn't put it past her.

She wanted this divorce to happen so badly. I wasn't in any rush, but she was. Could she have gone behind my back? Or did Amanda go behind my back and speak to a lawyer and knew what she was entitled to?

"Well, respond to her?" Rebecca whined.

"What do I say?"

"Just say 'okay, what time.'" Rebecca rolled her eyes. "She's making it easy for you. Either accept her agreement, suggest a new agreement or go to a lawyer. Like really. Stop being so lazy."

With a heavy sigh, I picked up my phone. *Okay, how about this afternoon around three.*

"There you go, taking charge." Rebecca beamed. "Tell her, instead of letting her dictate everything."

I'll drop it off right now. I'm five minutes away.

I shut off the phone. "Well, I guess it's happening now." I wondered what she had brought me. And why now? Why the change of plan?

Before I had a moment to think, I got another message. *I'm outside.*

I stared at Rebecca. "How about you go get changed and dressed up, and after I get whatever she brought me, I'll take you out to dinner—just you and I." I placed a kiss on her forehead. "I love you."

She threw her arms around me and hugged me tight. "I love you, too. Don't take too long. Okay."

I'm coming, I texted.

I kissed Rebecca one last time before grabbing my shoes. *Here goes nothing.* I opened the door into the hallway and padded toward the elevator. Outside, by the front security gate, Amanda's car was parked on the street. She got out of the driver's seat.

She looked great today. She had her hair done, a form fitting jacket and tight jeans on. I found a small smile forming. *Why hadn't she looked that great when we were together?* I shook my head. I shouldn't be having these thoughts. Not anymore.

"Hi." I glanced into the back seat to check for Joy, but didn't see her. "Where's the baby?"

"With my mom." Amanda leaned against the fence. "You can pick her up from daycare tomorrow as agreed upon."

"Okay," I said, cautious that she was being so amicable.

Amanda turned and opened her back passenger door. "I don't have a lot of time." She struggled to take a large box out of her backseat and handed it to me. "There's a letter inside. If you don't agree, then we'll set up mediation and further negotiations through lawyers." Amanda bit her lip but appeared to keep herself relatively together.

What was this? Amanda was falling over in grief every time I saw her, but now she was all business?

"Did someone talk to you?" I asked.

Amanda shook her head. "I've merely accepted things. Make sure to review the letter and get back to me. Have a good day, Matthew." With a crooked smile, she turned and got back in her car.

She drove away.

I stood there, holding the box. What was that? I turned toward the gate, propping the box on my knee as I put in the code to open the door. What the hell did she pack?

Inside the house I plopped the box on the table as

Rebecca entered the kitchen. "Oh, that didn't take you long?"

"No, it didn't." I stared at Rebecca who had changed into a simple floral sun dress. I was looking forward to an easygoing afternoon.

"What's in the box?" she asked.

"She said a letter with what she wants, and a bunch of stuff. I'll check…"

"Why not check now, and then, we can go out," Rebecca pressed.

I sighed, as she wasn't giving me much of a choice. I opened the flap and picked up the white envelope. I tore it open, removing a typewritten letter. At the bottom was Amanda's signature in bright red, cursive writing. I always had a weird fondness for how she signed her name. She used to write me little love notes because she knew I loved her writing.

"What does it say?"

I looked at the letter and handed it to Rebecca.

From the box, I pulled out a black photo album with a pink flower on it. Rebecca put the letter down beside me as I opened it. I flipped through the photos of Ivory as a baby.

"Is that Joy?"

I shook my head. "Ivory." My voice was low. I kept flipping until I stopped at a picture of Ivory sitting in the sink, covered in chocolate. "She was eight months there. We were celebrating my mother's birthday. What was supposed to be a little taste." I laughed a bit and flipped to the next picture.

"She looks like she was a happy baby."

A shallow sigh escaped my lips. Every time I looked at

Joy, she reminded me of Ivory. We named Joy after Ivory's honor. It was ironic considering, when she was born, our lives were nothing but. I kept flipping through pictures until I came across a picture of Ivory and I.

Rebecca placed her hand on my shoulder. "That is a nice picture of the two of you."

I smiled. "She was a wonderful little girl. I-I miss her everyday."

I gently touched the outline of her face, while clenching my jaw. Even a year out, it still didn't get any easier. I closed the album. I couldn't look at any more photos of her. It was too much. I clenched my fist, before I set it aside. I reached in for something else, a brown envelope. Did I dare open it?

Rebecca wrapped her arm around my shoulder. "What's that, hun?"

"I'm not sure." I took a silent, deep breath, opened it and pulled out a newspaper. My heart dropped. I closed my eyes for a moment and let out a loud, moan-like sigh. It was an obituary for Ivory. Why didn't Amanda warn me that this stuff was in here? Some kind of warning, or something, would have been nice. I held the obituary in my trembling hand.

Rebecca took it from my hand. "Why don't we look at this later?"

I heard her but didn't move. Taking a break would be good, but I couldn't. I wanted to know what else was in the box. Amanda's voice echoed in my head. She told me I was running from my problems. She accused me of wanting to forget all about Ivory. So, that was what she was trying to do. Remind me of her. Remind me that no matter what, we had another daughter.

"I need to do this," I looked downward. "I need to do this. Find out what I want to keep ya know..." It wasn't the total truth. For some odd reason, maybe to ease some lingering guilt I wanted to unpack everything.

Next were some photos of Joy, an ultrasound photo of when Amanda was pregnant with Joy. I pulled out a photo of Ivory holding the ultrasound, with a sign saying, 'Big Sister'. Life was great then. We were happy. I was happy. I had it all... I closed my eyes, trying to forget about the car which hit my daughter — Took away my daughter. He fucked up every damn thing in my life. I clenched my fist and banged on the table. "I'm sorry, Ivory. I'm so sorry I wasn't there."

"Hun, it wasn't your fault."

I forced myself to make eye contact. "Then who's fault was it?"

Rebecca glared at me, her mouth twisted. "Amanda's."

I looked away, partly ashamed. I did blame Amanda. But she blamed me. I spent so many nights texting Rebecca and blaming Amanda. I told her that she left her out alone while I had to go to the backyard. There was so much resentment. Every time I looked at Amanda, I felt more rage. Now I wasn't angry anymore — just sad. Depressed. I would do anything to go back in time.

"I just wish I was there to save her..."

I stood from the table, without even making eye contact with Rebecca. I didn't care. I opened the fridge and grabbed a beer. Cracking it, I let the cool liquid slither down my throat. The can was half gone before I sat back down at the table. Out of the corner of my eye, I saw

Rebecca had her hands on her hips, her upper lip curled. I pretended not to notice as I glared at the box. I wanted to just open up the sliding door in the living room and dump it — over with. I wanted to dump any trace of the pain, of the memories, overboard. I slumped my shoulders. I couldn't' do that.

I took another swig, my mind conflicted. I just wanted to forget that day. I wanted to forget all about it.

Rebecca stood with her arms akimbo. "Drinking is not going to solve your problems."

I shook my head. She didn't know. How could she tell me what would solve my damn problems if she had never lost a child. Never had her marriage blown up. I sighed. Of course she understood. I dumped her. The good old, Matthew Talan, the piece of shit who broke her heart. I ignored her as I retrieved another beer.

Rebecca breathed heavily. A sign she was about to flip her lid. She was always getting mad over everything, even back when we first started dating.

I chugged back the tall beer and sat in front the box, pulling things out of it. I wasn't about to let these emotions consume me. I wasn't going to let Ivory's death or Rebecca get in my way. I was so sick of feeling sad, defeated.

I pulled out one of Ivory's baby blankets, then birthday cards, and tossed them on the table. My great grandmother had made this for me and she gave it to me a few years before Ivory was born. I guess it was fitting for it to be returned to me. Next was a birth announcement in the newspaper.

Rebecca put her hand on my arm, temporarily stopping me. "Hun, take a break."

I shook my head. "I need another beer."

Without another word, I kept going through the box. It was like self-torture or therapeutic. I didn't know. What I wanted was to reclaim myself.

Rebecca walked away from the table and into the living room. I guess I had to grab my own beer. I took the last sip of the can and grabbed another. Sitting back at the table. I reached in and pulled out a wedding invitation. My hands trembling, I looked to see if Rebecca was watching. She wasn't, so I quickly shoved it inside the photo album. I didn't want her to see.

I remembered the weeks leading up to breaking off our engagement. The week following meeting Amanda for the first time was the ticking bomb to the end. Rebecca was angry, so angry. She screamed in my face, threatening to call off the wedding. I bought Amanda a drink. That night, Rebecca made me sleep on the couch. I apologized, but I didn't mean it, because my every thought had been about her, about my wife. I kept fantasizing about kissing her. I started texting my friend to see if he could arrange for us to meet again.

I took a sip of my beer, my lips pinched. I never realized how unhappy I was. How unfair I was to Rebecca. She had a right to be mad. I was angry when Amanda fucked her boss. I was furious when I was doing the same thing. She and I exchanged jabs at one another. She called me a piece of crap for not being there, and I called her a slut. It wasn't my proudest moment. I had reached out to Rebecca, or she reached out to me. She saw the obituary in the newspaper and messaged me. I gave her my number. We texted. Amanda caught me. It devastated her. She retaliated and talked to, rather slept with, Roger.

My lips twisted. God, I hated that man. My fists clenched. He fucked my wife. He fucked in my bed, around my child.

"Matthew?"

I looked up in a haze. "Huh?"

"If you are going to sit around drinking all day, I'm going out."

Shamefaced, I glanced downward. "I'm sorry," I mumbled.

Rebecca gritted her teeth. I knew she was trying hard not to show her frustration.

"I'm sorry," I repeated. "I'll stop drinking. Just don't be mad."

"We were supposed to go out for lunch, but once again, Amanda, or something Amanda did, ruined that."

I shook my head. There she was, blaming Amanda again. It wasn't Mandy. It was me. I was the screw-up.

"There you go defending her again."

I stood. "I'm not defending her, Babe. I didn't say anything."

She grabbed her keys off the hook by the back patio door. "I'll be back. Please, for the love of God, stop drinking and put that shit away."

I bit my lip as my gaze averted to the box — the forsaken box.

"Okay."

Without another word she left. I heard the door close behind her. I took a deep breath and sat. A sense of relief grew over me. Later, I'd think of something to make it up to her. Maybe I'd buy her some flowers or chocolate or something. Small gifts always lifted her spirits.

Reaching in to see what else was in there, I fingered the velvet box. My heart skipped a beat, literally. I opened it up. It was my wedding band, with our wedding date engraved. I slipped it on my finger. I'm not sure why, since we were divorcing, but it felt like old times. I was happy to be her husband. I used to show her off, like a trophy wife, but she was so much more. Now, it felt hollow.

Ten years ago we got married. It was a simple wedding. None of that over-planning, no arguments and no stress. A complete opposite from wedding planning with Rebecca. The day I called it off with her, was the day after unloading all my problems onto Amanda.

I took the ring off as it meant nothing now. We weren't together and we'd would never be together again. She wanted a divorce. She told me so. I never tried to stop her or begged her, instead I moved in with Rebecca. We were together. It was how it was supposed to be. Just like ending my engagement with Rebecca back then was supposed to be. I shoved all the stuff into the box.

I took the box to the bedroom, shoved it in the far empty corner of the closet and lay back on the bed.

I flipped to Amanda's name in contacts. I wanted to text her that I accepted her terms, and that we could arrange to speak to a lawyer to get the papers drawn up, but I stopped. First things first, I needed to make up with Rebecca. I needed to start putting her first.

I love you, I texted Rebecca.

I waited for a response, when she responded back. *I love you, too.* Followed by: *I just wish you'd get over your wife. If you can't move on, then maybe you should just go back to her.*

My mouth opened slightly, as I responded. *I want to be with you.*

I closed out of her name and stared at the ceiling. She was right I needed to get over Amanda. Soon, it be would be over. Soon, I'd start over with Rebecca. We used to be in love. At least when we first met. She had a nice smile, and had great taste in fashion and cuisine. We bonded over our love of trying new and exotic foods.

Why was ending it so hard? Why was I thinking about Amanda at all?

10

I left the lawyer's office, clutching the divorce papers. I couldn't believe this was really happening. I was leaving my wife—legally. Amanda hadn't said much to me since dropping off the box of mementos and memories. I still couldn't figure out if it was her way of telling me something, or trying to make me doubt my feelings. Either way, I second-guessed myself. Why was I so confused? My wife technically dumped *me*. But why didn't it feel like that? The big question was, why was I even thinking about her, period?

I slouched into the seat of my car. A tremendous weight rested on my shoulders—the mountain of paperwork I had to do tonight from slacking at work. My mind flitted all over the place. This whole divorce, maintaining peace with my girlfriend, and becoming a part-time father had took a shit on my life.

I fiddled with my collar and ran my hand through my hair. I was surprised Rebecca hadn't bitched about me getting a haircut yet. She seemed to always complain about something, but it was understandable. She was on pins and needles. I kept promising to finalize this divorce, but, for one reason or another, I remained married. I was still stalling.

I drove from the courthouse. Instead of going home or to Amanda's to drop off these damn papers, I cruised around. I wasn't in the mood for a lecture. I could hear

Rebecca chirping in one ear. *"Why are you stalling, Matthew? Just get divorced already."* In the other ear, it wasn't so much Amanda's voice as her tone. *"I need more time. Tell her to stop pressuring me."* I just wanted them to get along.

I pulled over to collect my thoughts. No matter how hard I tried, I couldn't get her from my head. When we lived together, we couldn't stand the sight of one another, and we were at each other's throats. Amanda pretty much kicked me out of the bed. Well, not in so many words, but it was implied.

I squeezed the steering wheel. "Why did you have to ask for this divorce?"

She couldn't hear me, but I needed to hear myself talk. Big ol' corporate man was losing his mind. Rebecca had told me this morning I was heading down a dark path. I groaned. My life went to shit when my daughter had died, when that goddamn piece of shit ran her down like she was nothing. I pounded a fist against the dash in frustration.

Then my phone vibrated. It always vibrated when I didn't want it to. I just wanted to be left the fuck alone. I sighed. It was Amanda.

What? I texted without reading the message. Not sure why.

Jeez. I was just asking, Amanda replied a moment later.

I felt like an asshole. If I had taken my head out of my ass and read her message before jumping down her throat, I would not have come across as some jerk. *Are you still coming by?*

I didn't want her to come by but I kind of did. I wanted to finalize this divorce. I wanted to be a divorced man with one less woman controlling my life, my thoughts, and my heart. What I really needed was a drink. Instead, I responded, *How about now?*

It'd be quick. I'd drive over there, get out of my car, hand her the paperwork, tell her to sign it and we'd file it. It'd be strictly business, like I do all day long. Easy peasy.

I felt a bit better at the little plan I had formulated. *Okay, sounds good.*

It comforted me that she was onboard. If we went back a few months ago, I would have thought she would have elongated this whole divorce for as long as possible in an attempt to punish me. She had been so angry.

I arrived at the house. Inside the living room window, the blinds were slightly open, revealing a pacing Amanda. A tickle formed in my throat, a familiar feeling one too many times. I knocked on the door before attempting to open it again. As I expected—but never would get used to—she had locked the door.

Moments later, the front door opened, and Amanda let me in. I held the orange envelope containing the summons.

Amanda's gaze fixated on it as she bit her lip and hunched. "So that's it then?"

I was surprised to see tears forming in her eyes. "Yeah."

"It's all over." A tear ran from her left eye.

I couldn't bear to see her cry, even if Rebecca was right, and it was all over. I set the envelope on the foyer table and hugged Amanda.

She gasped but didn't resist and lay her head on my chest. We said nothing else. What was there to say? I was here to have her sign away our marriage. I was so sure it'd be in and out, but now I wasn't.

When we pulled apart, I saw what I thought was Amanda's smile for a brief moment. My heart skipped a beat. I smiled back.

Amanda reached for the envelope. "So … this it?"

I nodded.

Amanda stared at the envelope, shaking. A twinge of guilt emerged. She opened her mouth to speak but stopped, then changed the subject. "Do you want something to drink?"

Knowing I really shouldn't but that I needed it, I accepted. Maybe I wanted to spend one more time with Amanda, my wife, while she was still my wife. Maybe it would end some of the pent-up guilt I had about our marriage's demise.

I sat at the oak table in the dining area adjacent to the kitchen. My great-grandmother had bequeathed it to me. I had chosen it from all her things when she had passed, because Amanda had liked antique things. What better thing then to have a two-hundred-year-old sturdy oak table? Amanda had been so happy, which had made me happy.

Amanda brought me my favorite brand of beer and opened a soda for herself. Maybe she still thought about me on some level. Either way, it was the last thing I needed, but I wouldn't refuse it.

"So, where's Joy?" I asked.

"She's sleeping. I'll be sure to wake her up before you leave so you can say hi."

My legs shuffled as I took a sip. "I'd like that."

Amanda sat a few feet from me, playing with her hair

and sporting that same jaded, blank glare she had so many times in the months leading to asking me for a divorce — the look of desperation and the look of not knowing where to go. I had been too focused on Rebecca to really notice just how conflicted Amanda had been. If she hadn't pulled the plug, I'd probably still be living here, but Rebecca would still be my mistress, my side piece. I cringed at that thought. She deserved much more than that. She deserved to have me, free *and* divorced.

Amanda took a sip. "So, how've you been?"

"All right. And you?"

There was a long pause. "I broke it off with Roger." She shook her head. "Not that it matters."

I clenched the glass beer bottle. That guilt creeped up again. It shouldn't matter, but it did. I was glad to hear she wasn't seeing that piece of shit. When I found out she was seeing him, I got angry. I fumed. I called her a whore. I called her a slut. I told her many times, almost encouraged her, to go be with her lover. Yet I did the same thing. It wasn't my proudest moment. Maybe that was why I felt so guilty. I was a hypocrite.

"Sorry," she muttered.

I reached over and caressed her shoulder. "Don't be …" I looked away, ashamed, coward-like. "I'm the one who should apologize." I took a deep breath. "I shouldn't be making this hard. I can't hide it." I pulled away. "I'm glad. I'm glad you aren't seeing him anymore." My heart stammered. What was I doing? Why was I telling her that?

Amanda clenched her jaw.

"I'm sorry."

"Is this really what you want? What we want?"

I flinched, as her question caught me off guard. "What do you mean?"

Her face filled with tears. "I-I just wish things would have been different." She wiped away the tears. "Ivory should be alive. We were supposed to be a family. All four of us. Then—" She stood. "Never mind."

"What were you going to say?"

"Then she came into the picture. Rebecca. She's making this hard. She's pushing you to make decisions before you're ready. She …"

I reached in and quickly pulled Amanda toward me and kissed her.

She recoiled, taken aback.

I looked away. I didn't want an argument. I wanted to appease her, like I do for Rebecca all the time. But I couldn't deny it felt good, almost felt *right* after all these months.

"What was that?" Amanda whispered.

"Nothing."

Amanda placed her hand on her hips. "Don't tell me nothing."

"It really was. It was a miss—" I stuttered. "Um, misunderstanding."

Amanda's lips curled, her stature strong. "Bullshit!" A glimpse of her fire emerged. "Don't tell me nothing. You don't just come in here and kiss me and tell me it's nothing!"

"It—"

"Stop lying! It wasn't a misunderstanding. It was deliberate. What do you want?"

I couldn't muster a response.

"So you want me to be your new paramour?"

I shook my head. "No!"

"Then what is it?"

Amanda pushed me into a corner, and I didn't know what to say. If I told her the truth, she'd be crushed. If I said nothing, she'd paint this picture, this unrealistic scenario.

"Why don't you go be with your *girlfriend*?"

"No!"

Amanda's mouth opened wide, and I'm sure mine did too. What was that? After an awkward moment, she reached over and kissed me back. I didn't resist. I let it linger. I pulled her head closer, and the kiss remained.

"Is it still nothing?" she asked. "Because for me, it was sure thrilling."

"Oh?"

Her coy response aggravated me. One minute she was pissed and the next she was flirting. Or was she testing me?

Amanda paced in long strides, like a prosecutor grilling a defendant on the stand. "Are you surprised?"

I fumbled for my words. "Um, no." I swallowed in a big *gulp*, but I was surprised.

I was still lying to Amanda. I've been doing a lot of that lately. I couldn't be straight with my girlfriend, and I couldn't tell Amanda the truth if my life depended on it. I was selfish. I didn't want to be the bad guy. That was the real truth.

She frowned. "I'll just sign the papers. I won't keep you."

My mouth opened to object, but what was stopping me?

"Unless you don't want to."

I knew Amanda was talking in circles, playing mind games with me. What was with women and manipulating my feelings?

Amanda grimaced. "Then what the hell do you want? You're sitting there with a dumb look on your face. Why did you agree to stay at all?" She twirled her finger around her hair and glared at me. "Well?"

I chugged the last of my beer and, once again, leaned in to kiss her before she had a chance to speak.

Amanda blocked my attempt. "Why are you avoiding the question?"

My lips parted.

"Well?"

"I could ask you the same thing? Why did you invite me in?" I stroked the back of my neck. An appreciative sigh escaped my lips. It was a relief to flip the question onto her.

Amanda frowned.

"So now who is avoiding the question?"

Amanda clenched her jaw. "Why are you being a jerk?"

I almost wanted to roll my eyes but didn't because I didn't want to offend her. She was one to talk, but I had learned to bite my tongue.

"No, seriously."

"I'm not."

"How would Rebecca feel about you kissing me?"

I shrugged. "She doesn't need to know."

"So, you're lying to her."

I paused. She got me. I was lying. I was hiding from Rebecca. I don't even know if Amanda really cared so much, as she wanted to be right—she despised lying—And

I had lied. I had lied about having another woman before she discovered the texts between Rebecca and me. I had tried to gaslight her when she discovered it, and I had tried to convince her we were just friends. But she didn't believe it. She had told me — with those striking eyes once able to sweep me off my feet — that she knew I was lying, soon after she had started an affair with Roger. She hadn't lied about it. She had told me that she wanted to feel loved, that I hadn't been there for her--but she hadn't been there for me either.

"I told her I was coming by here." A partial truth seemed better than nothing.

Amanda rolled her eyes. "Try being honest. Not for me, not for her, but for yourself."

I dropped my head. "Okay."

Amanda placed a finger under my chin. "You can start by being honest about why you're lying to Rebecca."

I sighed. "I told her I was coming here to get the divorce papers signed. That isn't a lie. I didn't expect to stay here so long."

"So what changed?"

I decided honesty was my best option, because, in the blink of an eye, Amanda could change and make my life a living hell. I didn't want to be on her bad side. "I just wanted to spend one last afternoon with you as my wife. I didn't plan on it, but you invited me in, and I just agreed." I reached for the empty beer bottle. "You even kept my favorite beer on hand."

Amanda grinned. "It's habit. I have a whole case you can take with you if you want."

"So, while we're being honest, Mandy, why don't you

tell me why you invited me in?"

Her whole disposition changed. Melancholy crossed her face. "I missed you." She darted past me. "It's hard just to let someone you spent so long with go. Even when I'm pissed at you, I keep wishing you were here." She bit her lip. "Is that honest enough for you?"

A wave of shame overcame me. I took one of her hands gently into mine. "Tragedy and lies was what brought us to this point. Believe it or not, I just want you to be happy, Mandy." My gaze locked with hers.

Her eyes looked as racy as the day I had met her. She was vulnerable, just like the girl she had been when she had forgotten her wallet at the bar. I had come to her rescue, and I was smitten.

I took a heavy breath, avoiding her stare. "The truth is, I think about you every day." For the life of me, I suddenly didn't know why, especially since we were divorcing.

"Me too," she murmured, her voice hoarse.

I met her gaze. My heartbeat sped swiftly. An intense cold shiver ran down my spine. My heart filled with a longing. It'd been a long time since I had felt this way. Pieces of my wife I thought had been long forgotten resurfaced.

Amanda bit her lower lip as she beamed at me, drawing me in.

Without hesitation, I reached in and laid a kiss on her soft lips. It tasted sweet, almost like how I remembered them.

Amanda returned the kiss, this time pulling the back of my head closer.

I didn't resist. My conscience screamed, *No, terrible idea, this should end.*

I realized then I knew four things. I could tick them off in my head. We were divorcing. I was with Rebecca. I had promised Mr. and Mrs. Larsen I wouldn't hurt their daughter again. And here I was doing just that. But I couldn't pull away. She was my wife, and, from a legal angle, we were doing what married couples did.

Sweat glinted on my forehand.

She gently worked her tongue into my mouth.

I couldn't contain myself. This was the first time since Ivory had passed that Amanda was letting me in emotionally after we had shut one another out. I wrapped my arms around her midriff and drew her toward me. I broke the kiss and worked my hands along her jaw and up her ear.

She let out a soft lament as my hands caressed her back. Her fingers entwined in my hair. She smiled from cheek to cheek as she reached for my pants, undoing the top button.

I tried to step backward. A part of me knew this was wrong. I had come here for a purpose, to end my marriage. Instead, she was sucking me back in. It felt right, but so wrong.

Amanda reached in again and locked her lips with mine.

As my mind fought with itself, my hand fumbled for Amanda's blouse. I unbuttoned the first button, then the second, and third. I was excited. Guilty, but excited.

Just as I unbuttoned the last one, my phone vibrated.

We stopped and stared at one another, both breathing heavy, the desire raging.

She paused before she furrowed her brow. "Do you have to?"

I took a deep breath as I reached for my phone. It was a text from Rebecca, asking when I would be home. I felt a mass weighing me down. I gently pushed away Amanda.

"What have I done?" I whispered to myself.

Amanda touched my hand. The worst part was I didn't want to leave, but I had to. I couldn't cheat on Rebecca. It was one of the reasons why my marriage had turned to shit, and I couldn't do it to Rebecca. I couldn't hurt her again. My mind screamed that I still loved Mandy too. I couldn't deal with that right now.

I shook my head, trying to clear it, and buttoned my pants. "I can't do this. I'm sorry." Then I mumbled to myself, "I'm with Rebecca. I can't do this to her."

Amanda's eyes welled with tears as she hugged herself. "But ... I thought—"

"I'm sorry," I muttered again. "I know it doesn't mean much."

She didn't respond.

What have I done?

All I had to do was come here, get her to sign those damn papers and then leave, but I fucked that up. All I did these days was fuck up. I fucked up my marriage. I continued to fuck with my wife. I was breaking promises to my girlfriend. *I* was fucked up.

I needed a drink, but I didn't leave. I wanted to make sure Amanda was all right. Not that anything I could do would help.

"Please stay," she begged.

"Please let me go. Just let me go." My guilt ate me

alive. It would be so much easier if she told me to scram. "You deserve to be happy. Just not with me."

"Fine."

"Fine?"

"Are you going to run again? Leave me, break my heart all over again? Fine, Matthew, do it. I can take it. But just know, if you come back, I ..."

I hurried for the door, turning my back on the women I'd hurt, wondering if she knew my heart was just as broken. I glanced at my phone. If Rebecca hadn't texted me, no doubt I would have gone through with it.

I texted Rebecca, telling her I was on my way.

Half way home, I realized I hadn't said hello to Joy. My chest fell. I guessed I could add *shitty father* to the list of things I had done wrong today.

11

I kissed Rebecca goodbye before heading to work. I had sent her flowers and chocolate and had even planned a date tonight to compensate, I told myself, for what I had done the other night.

I blinked, swallowing to ease my dry throat. I tossed and turned last night and woke exhausted. This time, not because of the usual thoughts about Ivory but because of Amanda. I had enjoyed it. I had enjoyed the kiss and being around her. I had to fight the urge to fall back into old familiarities.

I inhaled. And then exhaled. If only Rebecca hadn't messaged me, I would have gone through with it. No matter how hard I tried to do the right thing, I screwed up everything. Now I had to convince Amanda to sign those divorce papers, keep Rebecca happy, and prevent Amanda from telling her about what had happened or what was about to happen.

So far so good.

I arrived in the parking lot and found my spot. I sat for a moment to tighten my resolve — today would be just another day. Maybe I could find an excuse to stay late. I could stop for a drink before taking Rebecca on our date. It even crossed my mind to plan an extravagant vacation just to escape my fucked-up life.

I retrieved my suitcase from the back seat and headed inside, strutting through the main doors as if life wasn't a nightmare right now. To the right was a water fountain, something Amanda admired. I mentally reprimanded myself as yet another thought of my wife formed in my mind.

"Good morning, Mr. Talan," the receptionist said as she came from behind the desk.

I faked a smile. "Good morning, Angela. How are you this morning?"

"I'm fine. And you?"

"Good." I glanced at my wristwatch. "I'd better go."

"Me as well."

I passed the desk to the west elevator. Hopefully, by next week, the east elevator would be operational. I had been on maintenance's ass about it, but the head of the department and human resources both had said it was out of their hands.

The elevator stopped on the sixth floor.

"Hey, Matt. Have you seen Rakin?" an employee in my wing asked.

I glanced at the row of cubicles leading to my office. Half of them sat empty.

"I'm sure he'll be here soon."

I sighed as I sauntered toward my office. Ever since Trey Gordon had become CEO, this place had fallen apart. Everyone took advantage of his incompetence.

Reports that were supposed to have been sent to the CEO yesterday sat on my desk. I called to the nearest employee in the cubicle. "Could you take these to Tray?"

"For sure."

I plopped into my leather chair and sighed. Where was my assistant? Please tell me she hadn't decide to take the day off with the rest of them. She always arrived before I did. But I was also a few minutes early, which was new for me. No one seemed to notice though, and, if they had, they didn't say anything.

I sat behind the large mahogany desk and logged onto the company computer. I was expecting an important email for a major retail project. My inbox was empty. I frowned. This was just my luck. With how my life was going, this would be just one more thing to add to my list of failures.

After I refreshed the browser a few times, Susan finally arrived through the door. "Good morning, Matthew."

"Good morning."

She frowned.

I realized my voice must be less chipper than usual.

Susan sat on a stool on the other side of the desk.

I rustled through a stack of papers in attempt to hide my disdain. "I haven't received a single response from the emails I had you send yesterday." I turned my attention to aimlessly clicking through screens, waiting for that email.

"I wonder what's taking them so long."

I stared at the screen and groaned. "I don't know."

I hoped my proposal didn't have any problems. The deadline approached, and I couldn't afford to make a mistake now, not when the rest of my forsaken life was in turmoil.

Susan glanced at me with concern in her eyes. "Is everything all right, Matthew?"

I shook my head. "I just have a headache. Don't worry." I forced a smile while, once again, refreshing the browser. "They told me by eight a.m. this morning," I mumbled.

"I could write a follow-up email for you."

"No. It's okay. I'll call them. I really need to step in and get this settled before I miss the deadline."

Susan didn't say anything.

It would be fine. I'd make a few calls, find out what was wrong and then focus on fixing the problem. At least my day job wasn't falling apart. Yet.

I dialed the number.

"Hello. Rod Philips' office. Diana speaking. How can I help you today?"

"Yeah. It's Matthew Talan. Can you patch me through to Phillips, please? It's urgent."

A slight pause. "Okay, I'll put you through."

"Thanks."

I drummed my finger on the table as that godawful annoying soft jazz music played through the phone.

Susan tapped my shoulder and mouthed, *Can I get you anything?*

"A coffee," I whispered, holding the receiver from my mouth. I wished I could have asked her to add a shot of something.

"Hello, Mr. Talan. How are you?"

"I'm good. I'm just calling about the proposal I had sent you yesterday afternoon for your review?"

Typing sounds came from the other end. "Yes. I received your email. But I only received one of the two documents required. I got the list of contacts but no proposal."

I took a deep breath. "Are you sure? There must be some kind of mistake, because I'm positive the proposal was sent."

"Well, I never received it. Why don't you send it over again, and I'll get on the phone with the investor and see if they'll wait until this afternoon to review the details. All right?"

I agreed, hung up the phone and ran a hand apprehensively through my hair. If he won't postpone, then I'm in real shit. Without wasting another moment, I sent another email to Rod Philips with the required documents.

Susan returned with my coffee. "Did you get it all figured out?"

"Yeah," I whispered, looking at the screen. "I hope."

"If you're ready, I can bring you the paperwork for the Johnson case."

I nodded. "Yeah. And please keep an eye on the inbox, and let me know immediately if you get a response."

"For sure."

The Johnson case had been back and forth with delay after delay but fortunately, no looming deadline, even though I wished there was one. It reminded me of my own life—an internal battle with myself, my wife, and my girlfriend.

My gaze darted to the browser. I prayed I would make the deadline for that project.

I skimmed through the first few pages. All the numbers seemed right. I took a drink of coffee and reached for my phone.

How's work <3, Rebecca had texted me.

I nearly spit a mouthful of coffee, the guilt creeping up again. *All right. Just a lot of paperwork. How about you?*

I just finished with a client.

Rebecca was a wedding planner, as ironic as that was. She rarely discussed her job, as much as she claimed to enjoy it. Maybe because it was so damn ironic. It felt like a slap in the face every time I came across a wedding magazine. Or maybe it was a slap to her face, since I had fucked her over. In general, weddings were nothing but a means to make money.

Do you have time for a quick lunch today? I responded.

A moment later, she replied, *Why? Something happen?*

I took a deep breath. I wasn't one who liked lunch, but the guilt, the feeling of making things right, rode my ass. *I just want to see my beautiful lady.* Rebecca always ate up all the cheesy lines.

All right. I have no appointments between 11am and 1pm.

I checked my calendar as Susan entered the room.

"I'm going to take an early lunch," I told Susan.

"All right, because you have a meeting at one."

I nodded. *How about we meet at 11:30?*

Susan brushed some hair from her face. "Got an appointment or something?"

I nodded. "No, just meeting Rebecca for lunch." I smiled, even though, deep in my gut, I felt like the biggest piece of shit.

Susan didn't notice, thank God.

"Before I forget, Rod Philip's office sent a follow-up email."

"Okay. Thanks, Sue."

She didn't immediately leave, but instead, stood fidgeting with some imaginary speck on her shirt.

"Anything else?"

"Are you finished reviewing the Johnson case files?"

I stared at the stack. "Yeah." I flipped to the last page and signed off on it. "You can file it, and take a quick break. Thanks."

Susan smiled and took the file from me. I trusted her judgement and everything looked good.

I checked the email.

TO: Matthew Talan, Finance Manager Dept.
FROM: Rod Philips
SUBJECT: Re: Investment Proposal

I got off the phone with our investors, as discussed in an earlier correspondence. He has agreed to postpone the meeting until tomorrow morning. I took a look at the proposal. If you could fax me a copy of the blueprint or have the contractor send a copy of the proposed blueprint by no later than 8am tomorrow morning, that'd be great.

Thanks.

Thank God it worked itself out. I leaned back in my chair and stared at a picture of Joy, donning a huge toothless smile, that sat beside my PC. My spirit lifted a bit. She was truly the only highlight in my life these days, the only person who didn't have an agenda or who I hadn't hurt … yet.

I ground my teeth. "I'll try to be a better father."

Susan entered the room, and I cleared my throat, hoping she hadn't heard me. "Sue, can you fax the blueprints to Rod Philip's office?"

"All right."

I grabbed my phone again. Today was a bit of a slower day anyway. Unfortunately, it was a bad thing, because it just made me antsier, crazier.

Amanda had texted me. *Are you picking up Joy today or would you rather tomorrow?*

Not one word about what had transpired. No matter how much I tried to convince myself, I couldn't keep her off my mind. I almost had sex with her, then I went home and had lied to Rebecca. Again.

Tomorrow.

As much as I wanted to see Joy, today wasn't a good day. I couldn't face Amanda and all the awkwardness that came with it. Not to mention I never took the divorce papers with me. I couldn't look her in the eye without her thinking I was this big, giant piece of shit, the man who messes with her emotions. I didn't want to be that man. I didn't want to hurt her anymore than I wanted to hurt Rebecca.

Someone knocked on the door.

"Come in," I said.

An employee who hadn't been here that long entered, and I still, for the life of me, couldn't remember his name—Andy or something?

"Do you have a minute?" he asked.

I glanced at the time. "Yeah. What can I do for you?"

"I can't get a hold of Rochelle regarding the art gallery project. Is there another contact I can call, because I need to run an issue that just came up?"

I twirled in my chair for a moment. "Did you try calling the project manager?"

"Yeah. I left a message."

I frowned. I was so glad I had delegated that project to another, because Rochelle was always challenging to get a hold of.

I looked up Rochelle's email in my contacts and wrote it down. "Here. Email her, and, if you haven't yet, leave a message. All you can do is wait until she gets it unless the project manager gets back to you."

I had a pretty easy workload this week. I had closed on two projects and hopefully secured the investment for the condo upgrade. Maybe I'd take some time off and spend some time with Joy, maybe take a vacation—a much-needed vacation.

Soon, eleven o'clock arrived, and I packed up for an early lunch. I exited the elevator and approached the front door when Angela stopped me again. "Leaving so suddenly?"

"I'm just taking an early lunch."

"See you soon."

I scrambled for my car. I didn't waste any time like I usually did sitting in the parking lot. I arrived at the rendezvous restaurant before Rebecca did.

A moment later, she pulled up.

I scurried from my vehicle, lips parted as I glanced at her.

She smiled as she approached.

I planted a kiss on her forehead.

She skimmed her fingertips along my jawline, her eyes wide and bright. We didn't say anything to one another. When we had first dated before I had met Amanda, she always had this radiant glow about her. She could speak to you through the glint in her eyes. Even when she was furious, that aura overpowered me, almost scary-like.

I looked away, my body trembling.

Rebecca placed my face in her hands and forced eye

contact. "What's on your mind, babe?" Her words were soft, not annoyed or angry like she had been.

I swallowed. "Just a long morning."

Rebecca wrapped her arms around my upper body. "Why don't you tell me all about it over lunch, all right?"

I nodded. I had to keep in mind that this was how relationships went. We made small talk or talked about our everyday problems. It wasn't all rainbows like it had been when we first reconnected.

I staggered behind her.

We entered the Italian restaurant and sat near a window, allowing in a lot of natural bright light — a must for Rebecca.

The waitress brought us a menu and filled our glasses of water.

I studied the menu before settling on a stuffed cheese ravioli and rosé sauce. I closed the menu. "Have you decided, dear?"

"I think I'll get the caprese salad."

The waiter took our order, and we sat in silence.

Rebecca took my trembling hands into hers again. "What's wrong?" Her voice sounded more concerned than before.

I almost wished she was pissed, then I wouldn't feel like shit. "I'm just stressed with work." Here I was again, lying.

"Why don't we take some time off?" She donned a grand smile as she looked right at me. "How does that sound? You and me? We've been fighting a lot lately, and it's obvious it's been taking its toll. So why don't we both take off a few extra days and unwind?"

"Well, I did think of that earlier." Had she read my mind? "Where would you like to go?" I rubbed the back of my neck.

"How about Vegas?"

I played with the collar of my shirt. Las Vegas was the last place Amanda and I had vacationed before the accident.

Rebecca brushed some hair from her face and grimaced. "Well? Give me an answer."

"I don't really want to do Vegas." I wanted to go on a vacation but not to the place where my mind would be on my wife.

Rebecca's posture tightened. "Well, why not?" Her voice was harsh, and the frown lines on her face wrinkled. "You promised me when we got together you'd take me to Vegas."

I didn't respond, as I tried to formulate a response. She always got her way when we used to go on vacation. She usually chose the destination, the shows we saw, and even the food we ate. At first, it was a blessing to not have to plan, but, the more control I gave her, the more controlling she became.

"My God, Matthew. Why are you acting like this?"

A few patrons turned to look at us.

"*Shh!* You're making a scene. Let's talk about this calmly."

She sighed. "Fine. Tell me why you don't want to go to Vegas."

The waiter delivered our food, giving me a much-needed moment to formulate an excuse.

After Rebecca shoved a few mouthfuls of food in her

mouth, forcibly, she finally swallowed. "I'm waiting."

"Everybody goes to Vegas."

She planted her elbows on the table in fists. "Everybody but you and I." She clenched her jaw. "Did you take Amanda to Vegas?"

I sighed. "A long time ago. But it doesn't matter."

She rolled her eyes, sarcasm dripping from her lips. "Why do you let her dictate everything you do?"

I rolled up my sleeves. "She isn't. You are." I instantly regretted my words. "I'm sorry. I just don't want to go to Vegas. I want to go somewhere neither of us have been. Is that wrong?"

She put down her fork as she stood. "I'm going to the bathroom. Pick a place you want to go, and let me know when I get back."

She returned a moment later.

"How about Castle Rock?" I asked. "There's a lot of outlet stores, and it's a short flight."

"*Ugh!* I hate shopping with poor people. Who am I? Your wife?"

"What is that supposed to mean?"

She reached for my hand. "Don't be mad, babe. I didn't mean it."

"Okay, fine. You just make it seem like being married is a bad thing."

She smirked. "Also, I must know, did you ever take Amanda there?"

"No." It was on our bucket list, but we never made it.

"Okay, so Castle Rock it is." She kissed me, sealing the deal.

We sat in silence as I picked at my food. I didn't want

Amanda to be the topic of discussion whenever we planned anything or did something. Rebecca shouldn't be mad at Amanda, when *I'm* the one who dumped her. I hated walking on eggshells around her.

"Are you going to eat?" she asked.

I forced a mouthful. "So how was your morning going?"

Rebecca put down her fork, an indication she had a story to tell. Maybe something interesting, I hoped.

"Okay, you know Amy, right?"

I nodded. "Bridezilla?"

"Yes." She sighed. "You can't believe how difficult it is to please that woman."

Pleasing women, in general, was difficult.

"What did she do this time?"

"She changed the theme of her entire reception with the wedding six weeks away. Now she wants a mermaid theme. A little juvenile, but more money for me."

"So how are you going to pull that off?" I asked as I swallowed another bite.

Rebecca shrugged. "It shouldn't be too hard."

"Is there anything I can do to help?"

She laughed. "No, I'm fine. Besides, I don't think you and glitter match a lot."

"After having two—I mean—a daughter, glitter is nothing." I bit my lip. It never got easier.

"We really need to discuss turning the spare bedroom into a bedroom for Joy. I know you turned it down before, but it might be good for you—for us."

"Soon. Maybe after our trip."

The last thing I wanted to do was renovate another

little girl's bedroom. Twice had been twice too many, and it used to be Amanda's and my thing. I wanted to create new memories with Rebecca, and this wasn't the way I wanted to do it.

Rebecca heaved a sigh. "What can I do?"

"Huh?"

Her eyes were wet with tears. "No matter what I do, it's not enough. You're thinking about Amanda aren't you?"

"No," I lied.

"Then why won't you let me in. Why are you keeping me at a distance?"

"It's not like that—"

"I just feel like you're using me as a Plan-B," she interrupted, annoying me. "Like, you're waiting for that woman to take you back. It's sad. It's pathetic."

I chose Rebecca. I had walked away from Amanda. If that wasn't proof that she was my first choice, nothing else was.

I gulped and drank deeply from the water. I wished for something stronger as I prepared carefully chosen words. "*You* are my choice, so let's not talk about Amanda or my divorce. Let's talk about us. I love you. And only you." Even as I said the words, they tasted bitter in my mouth. Because it wasn't the entire truth. I loved my wife, even if I was trying to convince myself otherwise.

"Okay, fine."

I took a deep breath. "Tonight, let's go out and have a good time. We will leave work and personal shit at home and go out and have a good time like back in the days."

Maybe if I tried to recreate how things were when we

first met, I could really remember what it was that made me love her in the first place. We used to be fun. There was no pressure to grow up. We were in love at one point. Maybe if I could remind her and myself of that, I could finally let her in. Then I could let my feelings for my wife go. Because right now I couldn't deny it. I loved Amanda. And if I wasn't careful, I would lose them both.

From What's Broken

Part Three
Matthew

12

Tonight was the night I was going to take my life back. If Matthew could move on, then so could I. Didn't Joy deserve a mother who was happy? I didn't know why I expected anything different. I had to stop sitting around feeling sorry for myself. That was what I had to tell myself every morning lately. Matthew's rejection felt like a stab right in the chest, and it made me realize he wasn't the man I married. I knew he was gone, and I knew our marriage was done. It still stung like a bee sting, and it left a bitter taste in my mouth. I took a swig of my cold soda, and the liquid slithered down my throat like a snake. I let out a loud, wet burp without a care in the world. I needed to move on.

I texted Matthew to remind him to pick up some formula for Joy. I found it harder and harder to pump enough milk for her these days. My supply had dropped, and I frankly started to pump less. I had accepted my husband didn't want me and I had to let him go. I had to let go of the outcome. I knew I used breastfeeding as a means to try for control, and it wasn't right. If he wanted to be happy, even if it was with Rebecca, then I'd accept it.

Matthew responded with a simple *okay*. Ever since that night, he had been keeping his conversations with me short and curt. Clearly he didn't want me to spill the beans of our close sexual encounter. That made sense. The guilt would eat him alive. He'd probably be drinking or sucking up.

R.M. Demeester

That was his go to. Oh well, it wasn't my problem.

I turned around to face the wall length mirror. I slipped out of my t-shirt and jeans, kicking them to the rear of the bed, and slipped into a purple, short sleeved dress that hit an inch above the knee. These days that was as 'sexy' as I was willing be. I sported on the conservative side of dress. I had some curves brought on by two pregnancies, but besides that, I wanted to stay true to myself. Then I remembered Hank, the man I was about to go on a date with tonight.

Almost a week after Matthew and my last intimate, never to be spoken of, moment, I was grocery shopping with Joy.

It was so cliché, if there was ever a scenario of how two people met. I was grabbing some ice cream from the freezer, and without looking, I crashed right into Hank's cart. Both of us apologized profusely, and he smiled. He introduced himself and I did the same.

We started small talk. I was smitten, surprised that another man would even give me the time a day. Then we started talking about our kids. He had his son a few months older than Joy, and it seemed like an instant connection. He asked if I wanted to grab drinks some time and I said yes. So that led to nearly of week of texting. Now we had planned a date, and here I was.

At first, I told him I was single, but yesterday, I admitted I was separated, and he told me his divorce was final a few months prior. So we were both pretty new to the dating stage. I sighed, looking at his texts for the third time today. I wasn't really looking for a relationship.

I just wanted to move on, but I wasn't sure about him.

133

Hank was just the person I hoped would be able to do that. I just hoped he didn't get attached, or just want something sexual, like Roger. I didn't want a rebound relationship either.

At least, I had more in common with him than Roger. After all, we both had kids. Hank wasn't bad looking. He was tall, lanky, with big blue eyes, and a short brush cut. He was a few years younger than me, but he didn't seem bothered by that. He asked me what I liked to eat, and I told him Italian. He suggested a place downtown, and I agreed. I applied a little red lipstick to match my dress and pressed my lips together with a smile. I debated for a moment if I should put on some blush, but quickly decided against it. In the supermarket, I wasn't even wearing makeup and was still in my yoga pants, so I wanted to be myself. He could have more, maybe invite him to my house if we made it to a second date. There was more to me than just a pretty face.

I texted Hank, letting him know I was on my way to the café.

Sounds good, he replied, *I'll see you in a bit.*

Hank was more formal. Maybe too formal, but it was too early to determine that. I could say it was a nice change from the flirty and sexual texts between Roger and I. As I had expected, the moment I ended things with Roger, he would drop me. I hadn't had a text from him in weeks. Sure enough, less than a week later he found his new victim. Vanessa was some new little thing.

He flirted with her, telling her how beautiful she was and basically the same spiel he gave me, almost word for word. I bet though, by the end of the month, they'd be sleeping together. A metallic taste formed in my mouth, as thick bile accumulated in my throat. I sometimes wondered what I was thinking, expecting some kind of comfort. The reality was I knew he was a sleaze, and that he viewed me as nothing but a friend with benefits, but it still stung to be an afterthought.

I shook my head, breaking free of my floundering. I couldn't let Roger, Matthew, or my looming divorce control me anymore. I refused to let that ruin my night. Even if tonight went nowhere, I still knew I was desirable. I deserved that much.

I drove in silence, formulating in my head what I would talk about. The risk of some potential uncomfortable question would come up, but I guaranteed Joy would be brought up. I clenched my jaw. That would mean Ivory would be brought up.

I pulled up to the curb, my tire scraping the cement. An immense weight dropped on my shoulders and I quivered. As I left the house, I was semi confident. Ready. Excited. But now? I broke out in a cold sweat. Maybe it was too soon, but I couldn't not show up. Hank seemed like a good guy in the grocery store

I gulped as I opened the car door and got out. I stretched and took a deep breath. Everything would be alright. My hand trembled as I struggled to lock my car door. *Holy crap,* I thought to myself. *What if this goes badly and no man wants me ever again?* It wouldn't surprise me since my husband didn't want me..

Stop being silly, I tried to tell myself. It wasn't working.

I walked the half block to the little upscale café. It wasn't your typical café, it looked pricey. It was small, quaint and had the best calamari, or I was told. I opened the door, and sitting near the back was Hank. He was wearing a navy blue turtle neck shirt. I beamed. I always had a thing for men in turtle necks. It wasn't your usual everyday look. I had tried for years for Matthew to wear a turtle neck but he just refused.

Hank met me halfway to the table. "It's so nice to see you."

I smiled and little butterflies formed in my chest. "You too." He gave me a loose hug. An abundance of emotions pierced through me. Warmness radiated from head to toe. I just hoped Hank didn't expect something in return.

"Shall we sit down?" he asked.

I nodded sheepishly as we both took a seat facing one another.

"I hope you didn't have trouble finding the place."

I rubbed the back of my neck. Here came the small talk. "No. I have wanted to check out this place for a while. I heard the calamari was good."

He ran his left hand through his hair. "Oh, really?"

"Yeah. How did you hear about this place?"

"It is just a few blocks away from where I work. So, I come here for lunch often."

"Oh? So what do you do for work?" Under the table my legs trembled. I didn't know what else to really ask him. I was just taking his lead. I was so out of the loop from the dating scene.

"I'm a security manager. How about you?"

"I work at a call center."

Hank nodded. "So is that where you call people who didn't pay their bills?"

I chuckled a little. "Yeah." I tried to get a read on what he was thinking. He glanced at me assiduously so I took that as a good sign. A waitress approached the table. "Can I get you two anything to drink?"

"Can I get whatever beer is on special?" Hank asked.

I wondered if he was the cheap type.

The waitress stared at me. "I-I'll get a tea, please." I stuttered.

She walked away.

Hank's expression changed. "So," he was a little more serious now, "I remember you said you were separated from your husband in an earlier text. What's happening with that?"

"Yes," I started, a little put-off he would bring that up so quickly. I figured he just wanted to make sure I wasn't lying. "We have been separated for about four months now. Our divorce should be finalized soon." My voice sounded more jaded than I anticipated. I hoped Hank didn't notice, but I couldn't help it. The end of a marriage, no matter the circumstances, was hard. Especially when we shared so much history. "I'll be glad when it's over with," I added. I didn't know if my heart agreed with that statement just yet.

Hank frowned. "I know the feeling. I was so glad when my marriage ended. The divorce took longer than I was married to my son's mother."

I bit my lip. "I was married for ten years. I had two kids..." I trailed off, quickly reprimanding myself for my mistake in words. "How about we talk about something else? Talking about failed marriages is depressing, when I just want to have a good time."

The waitress returned with our drinks. "Have you two had a moment to look at the menu?"

"We need a few more minutes," Hank said.

The waitress bounced away cheerfully. On the inside, I felt relieved. She came at just the right time to rectify my mistake.

"What would you like to eat?"

I glanced at the menu. I was a bit low on cash so I scanned the menu for something affordable. "Hmm. I'll get the sirloin burger and parmesan fries with garlic aioli."

Hank chuckled. "You read my mind. That was what I was going to order, too."

"Good taste. What do you expect?"

Matthew was also a burger person. Every mini vacation he took me on before we got pregnant with Ivory, he ordered at least one burger. One time he ordered a liver burger, topped with onion rings. How I missed those days.

"I don't know."

I couldn't conceal my smile. "Me neither."

We made small talk for a few minutes before the waitress returned to take our order. After she left, we sat in silence for a minute.

"So, how old is your oldest?" Hank asked.

I gasped. I played with my collar, avoiding eye contact.

"You said you had two, right?"

I lowered my head. "Yeah. My oldest passed away last year." My mouth went dry, as a dark cloud surrounded me, sucking the energy out of the room.

"I'm so sorry." He reached over to touch my hand. I jumped.

"It's all right," I smiled, but it was rough and faded

quickly. "It was an accident. It was also the reason my marriage ended. But it's okay." I was repeating myself. *It would have to be okay. Nothing would bring back Ivory, and the sooner I started to accept that, the happier I would be. I'd always miss her.*

"I wouldn't have asked if I knew."

"Its fine, Hank. Really." As much as I wanted to forget all about it, I couldn't feel right leaving my date feeling guilty for the very thing I brought up. "I came to peace with it. Whether she is alive or not, she is still a part of me, and I have no shame talking about her."

He sighed. "Okay."

I felt a little better that it was out in the open. But I needed to quickly change the subject to something more positive, something that didn't involve my husband, my divorce, or my deceased daughter.

"So, do you like to travel?"

"Yes. I'd love to visit France someday. I never did make it there when I backpacked through Europe after I graduated."

"That'd be nice," I said noncommittally. Matthew and I had planned on travelling Europe one day. It was one of the things on our bucket list. For our second year marriage anniversary, we took a three week vacation to travel South America. We had an amazing time. A lot of pictures, hiking, and exploring. By day two I had sunburned, and he was there as my support. He was such a good husband.

"Where is the farthest you have travelled?" He asked me.

"Brazil."

"I hope one day to travel more. Maybe when my son is

old enough to enjoy it."

I had always wanted to take Joy to all the places I dreamt of growing up. "Me too. I just think of all the places I'd love to take Joy."

"It's a worthwhile goal. Maybe we could travel sometime, maybe."

The waitress brought our meal. Thank God, because it kind of sounded like he was already planning potentially traveling. I wasn't even sure if I wanted to be involved with anyone, never mind travelling with them.

"Thanks," I said.

I watched as he bit into his burger. He ate slowly, gracefully, almost. I was so glad he wasn't one of those guys who shoveled food in their mouth as if they hadn't eaten in a month.

He paused, peering at me. "Is something wrong with your burger?"

"No," I lied. I wasn't about to tell him I was admiring the way he ate. "It's just a bit too hot."

I quickly took a bigger bite then I normally would. I swallowed without hardly chewing.

"So, what do you do for fun?" I mumbled around my food.

I felt like this was an interview and I wasn't doing a very good job of making a good impression. More like I was trying to mask my insecurities and trying to change the subject instead of genuinely trying to get to know the guy. Maybe if I found out what he liked, maybe we could do something else, afterward. Fun, always determined if we would even get along, right?

"I like hiking and movies." He chuckled nervously.

"Kind of a simple guy."

"Simple is good." I wasn't ready to go home, and we were just about done eating, so maybe I can take this date further. Even if it didn't lead anywhere. "What do you think of a walk by the river?" I suggested. This was what I needed. I needed some simplicity. I needed even a night without my overcomplicated, overemotional life dragging me down.

"Sure, that's sounds good." Hank replied. "First we should finish eating, don't you think?"

"Oh, yes."

I stared down at my plate, while under the table my legs bounced foot to foot. Here's hoping a change of scenery could offer up some meaningful discussion. All night it seemed like my emotions were all over the place. One minute I was nervous as hell, the next I was kind of excited.

Hank took a bite of his burger and glanced seductively at me. I couldn't help but laugh. I bet he was enjoying or imagining something more than how tasty that burger was. My chest felt light, almost like I was on my way to cloud nine.

I managed to finish half my meal when I felt suddenly full. I pushed my plate forward and glanced at Hank. "I don't know about you, but I'm stuffed."

My subconscious was at work. I could have finished that burger, but I didn't. On my official first date with Matthew all those years ago, I had ordered a salad. I didn't want a salad but I wanted him to be impressed with me. Maybe that was what our marriage was based on, lust. Maybe that was what I was doing all over again, here with

Hank. Trying to compensate for something.

The waitress reached the table. "Can I get you guys anything else?"

"Just the bill," Hank said.

"Will that be together or separate?"

"I'll get it," he replied.

Before I had a chance to respond, he reached over and caressed my hand. My heartbeat sped up.

"Thanks," I stammered.

"I invited you to dinner. So it's on me."

"Thanks. I mean. I appreciate it."

"Besides, you suggested a nice walk by the river."

"Yes."

After the bill was paid, we stepped out of the cafe on the dimly lit street. The sun was setting, and it almost felt like the end of a date, but it was just the beginning, at least in my mind. Hank towered over me and I felt smaller than usual. My nerves were shot again.

"How about we meet in the parking lot across from the river? My friend owns the lot, so it'd be no problem."

I nodded. "Okay." At least he didn't insist on taking the same vehicle. On Matthew and my first, technically third, time hanging out, he picked me up. Here I was trying to avoid the same pattern. But it was so hard, when everything reminded me of my husband. The good, the bad, and the, well, ugly.

He reached in, and I reluctantly did the same, and we kissed. It was quick, unromantic, but he still smiled. "Meet you there, Amanda."

In the car I adjusted the side view mirror. I quickly checked my make up to see if I was still put together. I had spent so much time looking disheveled that I didn't bother to maintain my appearance.

I drove the short distance to the parking lot we agreed on. Hank was leaning against his car, waiting. He had put on a leather jacket, giving him a more 'tough' look that he didn't previous sport. I kind of dug it. It was different, so not Matthew.

He grinned when I got out of the car.

He held out his hand, with an intense glare. "Shall we?"

I accepted his grip as he guided me to a crosswalk. We walked until we reached the trails. He walked in the opposite direction from the cemetery.

"Nice weather tonight, hey?"

A slight smile formed. "Yeah."

I used to love to go for walks with Matthew and Ivory. She'd laugh, and stare out into the water, babbling and later talk about the scenery. How much I would love to go on family walks again, with Matthew. But it wouldn't feel the same. I closed my eyes as the image continued to form in my head.

Hank stopped abruptly. "Are you alright?" he asked.

I stopped my floundering, my unfocused gaze faltered. "Yeah."

"You just seem distracted?"

I relaxed my posture. "It's peaceful out here."

"It sure is." He glanced out into the horizon. "There is a park on the other side. Have you ever taken your daughter there?"

"I've walked past it sometimes."

He caressed my hand. "Maybe sometime we both take

our kids, as an outing. What do you say?"

I smiled. "I'd love that." Maybe creating some new memories with someone new, someone like Hank, was what I needed. Some kind of adventures that weren't tainted by death or by my cheating husband. Perhaps that was what Matthew was doing — trying to recreate new memories with Rebecca. They had history. Never mind how they broke up, and the small role I had in it. So maybe he just wanted a second chance to make it up to her, or maybe he just wanted some familiarity.

Hank and I walked a few miles, making small talk. He was so easy to talk too.

We arrived at a path, leading to the main road. "Would you like to stop for some hot chocolate before we walk back?" he asked.

"For sure."

At that moment it seemed like all the tension left my body. Warmth infused with my body. His offer was so simple, but it left an instant impression.

I followed him to the street where he bought us a hot-chocolate. The sun was setting, and the wind was picking up, so the warmth filled more than just my heart.

"Thanks," I muttered.

A quarter mile down the path, the mild chat, turned into more meaningful conversation.

"Are you interested in any particular type of music or sports?" Hank asked.

"I'm pretty open. Nothing offensive though. More wholesome lyrics." I didn't really like any particular artist or type of music, so I hoped he accepted my answer.

He nodded. "How about interests?"

My stomach fluttered. "I like to collect antiques."

He slowed down the pace. "Oh?"

"I have a degree in history. I used to be all into history, but life happened you know. Don't think about it as much as I used too. "

He rubbed his freeing hand through his hair. "So I take it you would enjoy going to the museum?"

A twinge of guilt emerged. We texted back and forth before even meeting, and not once did I mention my love of history.

"Yes," I replied with a little less enthusiasm than I just had before. "It's just been a while. But I'd like to go some time."

He smiled. "Is that an invitation?"

I giggled like a little school girl. "It could be."

"We can add it to the list of possible second dates."

My heart leaped in my chest. We were talking all night like a second date was possible, but it seemed like he wanted one. So many emotions were clashing around in my head. On the one hand, this was what I wanted. I tried to move on, and let my husband go. On the other hand, my heart was pulling in, too. Matthew and I once used to get along so well. We took walks, and he shared interest and support in history. The part of me that was a realist knew that I could find another man who could share the same interests as I did.

"Yes, that sounds wonderful."

But was it wonderful? My thoughts dripped in self-doubt. I had, for the most part, gotten over my anger had disappeared, and I accepted my role in the destruction of my marriage. It wasn't fair for me or to Hank for my issues to taint what should be fun.

When we finally reached where we had started, he stood a foot from me. "I had a good time."

I smiled. "I did too."

Without a word, he reached in and kissed me again. I grinned as I kissed him back. "Thanks for the nice evening."

He walked me back to my car. "I'll text you later."

"Sounds good."

Inside the car, I checked my messages before heading home. There were five missed calls from Matthew and a string of texts.

I quickly called him back.

"Hello, Mandy. About time you called."

A lump formed in my throat, and the frown lines on my forehead intensified. "I was busy. What's up?"

"Did you read my texts?"

"No, I saw the missed calls and called you."

"You need to come get Joy," he muttered.

"Why?" I twisted my hair around my fingers. "Is she hurt?"

There was a sigh, and some shouting in the background and Joy's cries.

"Why is she crying?"

He sighed. "I don't know, Mandy. But no matter what we try, she won't stop crying."

Tightness in my stomach unfolded tenfold. "Does she have a fever?"

"I don't know?"

I sighed and muttered some unkind words. "Fine, I'll come get her."

I hung up the phone and muttered. "He can't even take care of her for one night but wants more time. Seriously?"

I took a deep breath reminding myself that Matthew was a good father, but sometimes got overwhelmed with the crying. Or maybe it was Rebecca who couldn't handle the crying. Either way I needed to get to my baby.

Here I was having a decent night. Not that spending the night with Joy wasn't lovely, but I just wanted some time to recoup. I was hoping to go home, have a bath and binge on some of my favorite shows. Oh, and maybe text Hank some more.

I reached Matthew's street. I parked on the other side of the pool area.

I'm here. I texted Matthew.

A minute later he replied. *I'll bring her out. Where are you?*

Parked by the pool.

I set the phone in my lap and waited for Matthew to bring her down. I hope she wasn't catching yet another cold. Please, just let the only reason she won't stop crying is that she missed me because I couldn't afford to take off any more work.

Soon I saw Matthew come out with Joy in nothing but a onesie.

"Where is her jacket?" I asked him when I got out of the car.

He handed her over. "I'm sorry. I just didn't know what to do."

I held her to my chest, and her soft crying turned to hiccups. "There, there."

"Why isn't she dressed for the weather?" I asked again.

"She had no clean pants."

I sighed, as I set her into the car seat in the backseat.

"I hope I didn't interrupt anything important," Matthew said curtly.

I wanted to roll my eyes, but decided against it. "You kind of did, but it's fine." I turned to leave for the passenger seat when he stopped me. "What?"

"I'm sorry."

I combed my fingers through my hair. "It's fine. Have a good night."

I got into the car and glanced at a smiley Joy. At least she was in a better mood. Matthew tapped on my window. I rolled down the window.

"She really was crying."

I bit my lip. "Okay?"

"I just didn't want you to think, I was pawning her off. Because she was really crying all night long."

I took a deep breath. "I believe you. Don't overthink it. Have a good night."

I decided not to overthink it. I drove away. Halfway between Matthew and the house, my phone vibrated. I half expected it to be Matthew but was secretly hoping it was Hank.

I drove quicker, slightly speeding to get home, so I could relax and resume where I left off.

No sooner than I pulled into the driveway, I retrieved Joy and rushed inside.

I changed her diaper, put on a sleeper, and gave her a bottle. Inside the nursery, I lay her in bed and turned on the mobile. Here I was praying she fell asleep, so I could get a much-needed break.

I dimmed the lights and quickly exited the room. I waited outside her bedroom door for a moment, just in case she cried, but when she didn't I slipped back to the living room.

I plopped on the couch, resting my feet on the coffee table. I smiled. It was a text from Hank.

I had a good time. Did you?

Yes, I replied. *Sorry I didn't reply back sooner. I had to pick up Joy.*

I put the phone down and went into the kitchen to get something to drink. I poured myself a cup of steaming tea and returned to the living room. I returned to my conversation.

I thought you said, she wasn't supposed to be home tonight.

My stomach curdled. That was a response I often got from Roger when we planned. I took a deep breath, reminding myself that not everyone was like him.

Her dad wanted me to come pick her up.

I sipped my cup and waited for a response. My excitement was slowly dwindling. I hoped I was wrong though, and it were just my insecurities screaming?

My ex-wife had pulled that shit on me before, too. He replied.

It was evident he had a strong disdain for his son's mother. I didn't want that kind of co-parenting arrangement with Matthew. I wanted to be cordial. I just hoped him complaining of his ex-wife wasn't going to be a constant thing. That'd get old fast.

I'm sorry to hear. I replied.

They are exes for a reason. He texted, and a moment later. *I noticed you seemed a little sidetracked tonight. Just curious what that was about?*

My posture became rigid. *I was nervous. First date since my separation.*

I took a deep breath. He was digging too deep in my personal business, especially so soon in a potential relationship.

So you were thinking of your husband.

I bit my lip and lied. *No. Can we please talk about something else.* I replied. I took a deep breath before sending another text. *I just don't want to talk about my ex.*

I leaned back into the couch and took a deep breath. Why was he so interested in my marriage? We barely knew each other a week, went on one date, and he was asking me questions, that shouldn't even be a concern until we were officially dating.

My phone vibrated again.

Sorry. I really enjoyed hanging out. Why don't you let me take you out, and have a good time.

I sighed and replied. *All right. I had a good time too. A little fun sounds great.*

Sounds good, I'll text you tomorrow. Have a good night.

You too. I replied before shutting off my phone for the night.

13

I opened the fridge to retrieve the jug of milk. "I talked to the lawyer today."

"And?" Rebecca looked up from her phone, lips pressed together in a slight grimace.

"He thinks it'd be better to sign for a legal separation until Joy is over a year. Especially if I eventually go for more time with her."

Rebecca rolled her eyes. "Why don't you just demand more time now? You don't need a separation for that."

I brought my glass to the table and sat beside her. "He doesn't think I'd get more time until she is over a year because of her age." In the back of my mind, I wasn't sure I was equipped to take on more than I already was. Joy was needy.

The other night was the second time I had to ask Amanda to come pick up Joy because I couldn't stop her from crying. There was always the risk she could be documenting this. At least that is what the lawyer said. Never mind I was already going behind her back, and asking for advice from what was supposed to be a joint lawyer.

I felt like shit playing a fast one on her. I just couldn't stop Rebecca's constantly pestering. She hated that I didn't come home with the divorce papers and I had to lie to cover up another lie, and I was further into this mess. Now I felt like I had no choice but to ask for advice from the lawyer to appease her.

Rebecca put her phone down and released a deep breath. "Sorry." Her voice dripped with insecurity. "I just wish she wasn't such a big part of our life."

I reached for her hand. "I know, honey." I just didn't know how this was going to work in the long run. Amanda would always be a part of my life, especially with Joy being so young. We would be there for exchanges, events, and I didn't want to think about any of that.

"Why can't your divorce just happen already? Better yet, why should she get more time with Joy than you. She is an emotional single mother, where Joy would have more stability with two adults looking after her. I think the only reason she is trying so hard is because she wants child support out of you."

I rubbed my hand through my hair. "I can't control the system." Also, was Rebecca forgetting that neither one of us could get Joy to stop crying? Amanda, the single mother, was the only one who could calm her.

My phone vibrated. It was a text from Brent, a co-worker. *Hey, what's up, dude. Do you wanna go to the bar and watch the game in like an hour, bro?* I glanced sideways toward Rebecca. I wanted to go on my day off once in a while. I already knew she would want me to stay home. She always wanted my attention. Even with a child part time, I still seemed to be attached at her hip. When I was with Joy's mother, I got out more than this, especially when Ivory was alive. Amanda trusted me to go wherever and whenever I wanted.

"Who's that?" Rebecca asked briskly.

I swallowed hard. "Some guys from work."

She stood from the chair, her arms crossed. "Oh?"

I forced myself to make eye contact; her pose caused me instant discomfort. "They just invited me to go to the bar."

She narrowed her gaze. "And?"

"That's it." I paused. "Just to watch the game." I glanced away while I played with the collar of my shirt. I wanted to go. She had to know I wanted to go as well, based on how she was responding.

After a few moments I made eye contact with her.

Her posture was rigid. "What did you tell them?"

I shrugged my shoulders. "Nothing." I took a deep breath. "I wouldn't mind going, though." I inhaled, hoping she wouldn't freak out.

She gave a glassy stare. "So what am I supposed to do?"

"Huh?"

"While you leave me alone."

I wrapped my arms around her from behind. "I'll spend some time with you tonight when I get back, okay?"

She pushed herself forward, breaking my embrace. "Fine, whatever. Do what you want."

Uh-oh. What did that mean? "Don't be mad, Hun," I tried.

She turned her head. "I'm not mad."

But she was, and I felt on edge because of it. "I haven't been out with the guys in so long."

She nodded. "I know..." It was as if she wanted to say something but stopped herself.

"Why don't you go out with a friend," I suggested. "Buy yourself a new pair of shoes or something." Here I was hoping to butter her up to the idea so she wouldn't be mad, and I wouldn't go and come back to an angry girlfriend.

Ugh. Rebecca could hold a grudge and stay angry for a long time. I didn't want to make it a habit of bribing her into not being mad, but what choice did I have? She was being unreasonable, again.

"I guess I could go out," She mumbled.

I tried to hug her again but she shooed me away. "I love you."

"How late are you going to be?"

"No later than ten, as long as the game doesn't go into overtime."

She frowned. "Okay. Just don't get drunk."

I planted a kiss on her forehead. "I'll take a cab home, and tomorrow we'll do something. Whatever you want."

"Fine."

"Call up Sam or Julia. Maybe they would like to go for coffee or shopping."

"Okay. " She stood and left the kitchen without another word.

I stood for a moment, debating if I should go after her or just leave well enough alone. She said I could go, unhappily, but she still said it was fine. At this point, I'd either stay home with a woman who was pissed or go out and come home to a woman who was pissed. Seemed like a no brainer to me, but still, I felt guilty.

Okay I am in, I texted him back.

Brent worked as a manager over a different department, but he used to work in my department before he was promoted. I remember I had been given the first choice to switch departments but I didn't because it would have meant more work for the same pay, and I wasn't about to up my work load.

Sounds good, bud. See ya around six.

***

Showing up at the pub an hour before I was supposed to, I sat in the back corner by the pool table, sipping on a beer. I watched a man and woman playing a game of pool, laughing and having a good time. I'd never have dreamed of bringing Rebecca to play a game of pool. She would have bitched about breaking a nail or complained all the girls were fatter than she was. I shook my head. I didn't want to think about her right now. Amanda and I used to go to the billiard hall where she and I would team up against another couple and it was great. She was always more open to trying new things. She always showed me a good time. She was adventurous.

I grinned as I took a sip of beer. I wondered if she was thinking about me. When she picked up Joy she was dressed up, had she done that for me? No, I shook my head, of course she hadn't. Then why was she dressed up?

Did she … have a date?

The thought of her possibly going on a date with another man bothered me. I knocked back my beer in one gulp and ordered another. Boy, it had pissed me off when she started sleeping with her boss, and I was so nasty to her, but with good reason.

Now I realized I pushed her away and I wished I could go back and do things differently. I cupped the empty bottle in my hand tightly, my knuckles showing white. She was right. I hadn't been there for her, but I couldn't do anything about it now, right? Our marriage was over.

Or was it?

I finished that second beer and ordered another. I was less than an hour in, and I was on my third beer. My promise to Rebecca not to come home drunk wasn't going to happen, and I was definitely calling a cab later. I wondered if that was why she was so angry, why she, without coming out and saying it, didn't want me to go out. Maybe she was worried about me. Rightly so, I had been drinking more than usual lately, but I chalked it up to the stress between Amanda and I. Rebecca was a hard ass sometimes but she did care — she had to. When we first started talking again, she was there for me. She listened for hours while I laid on thick about how shitty my life had become. She was so understanding and told me she was there for me.

The first time I met up with her in person since reconnecting, I had just gotten back from a business trip, but lied to my wife about staying an extra night. Instead I spent all night and all day with Rebecca. We slept together, then that next morning we hiked. We ended the day when I took her to an expensive dinner and salsa dancing. I wasn't very good, but it was fun. We laughed. Her understanding wavered when I moved in with her. The understanding and listening ears turned into criticism. She no longer wanted to hear about my problems. She was pressuring me to end my marriage, to let go of the past.

I found myself with another empty bottle in front of me. I glanced at my phone. It was a few minutes until six. It was my cue to stop swimming in my own self-pity. This was the life I chose.

I left the table and headed for the bar, where I found

Brent, a frosty beer in hand.

He turned to me. "Hey, bro." As usual, he was in a polo shirt and khaki shorts. Brent only had two outfits, I think—a suit and tie for the office, and multiple polos and shorts. Typical.

"Hey." I suddenly felt like I was back in college. Brent was a professional by day but a frat wannabe by night with a family at home. Last year he'd invited me over for a hockey game, and his four-bedroom ranch-style house was impressive, as were the two grills and smokers on his brick patio that he, quote, "built with his own two hands like a real man."

I was starting to think Brent was less a frat boy and just a carefully dressed misogynist, the kind Rebecca prattled about hating, whatever that meant. I didn't really care.

"So, the old lady let you out?" Brent laughed and took a swig of his beverage.

"You could say that." A slow smile formed.

"Becky-Wecky has you on a short leash," he mocked, and though I should have bristled, I laughed with him. He chuckled loudly as he waved down the bartender behind the bar.

"What can I get for you, sir?" The young man asked.

"Can you get me a Corona? No lime this time, gives me an ulcer."

The bartender turned his attention to me. "What can I get for you?"

"Whatever is on special." I was going to be here a while, and it could get costly, but I didn't care. What was another domestic?

"So what happened with the Johnson case?" Brent

asked. "After Susan failed to send the proposal?"

The bartender returned with my beer and I handed him my card. "Keep it open," I told the young man and turned to Brent, a new beer in hand. "I managed to send him the necessary paperwork in time," I said, taking a smaller gulp this time. I had to start pacing myself. "His office approved the blueprints, eventually. I'm just waiting for the city to approve the permits and construction will start in the spring."

Brent nodded. "Right on, right on. I'd hate for that deal to go haywire."

I took a swig of my beer. "Tell me about it. It's a hundred-million-dollar project."

Brent threw a twenty on the bar. "Another please." He turned to me. "Do you know Laura over on third floor?"

I had run into her a few times. "The intern? What about her?"

He lowered his voice a bit. "She's been working out lately."

I leaned backward. So we were checking out women at the office. Fantastic. Maybe Rebecca was right about Brent after all.

My phone vibrated. It was a text from Rebecca. *What are you doing?*

I sighed and responded. *The game is about to start.*

I clicked out of the phone and slid it in my back pocket. "That the missus?"

I heaved a breath. "Yeah."

He shook his head in disbelief. "Ignore her."

I fiddled with the bottle. "I can't."

My phone vibrated again *and I stared at it. I'm bored. No*

one wanted to go shopping.

I stared at the screen thinking of a response.

Brent chuckled. "Man, does she have you whipped."

I opened my mouth to respond, but he was right. Rebecca had a lot of power over me. Her neediness was apparent.

Maybe watch a movie, I typed.

"Shut off the phone for a bit, man."

I fidgeted. "Yeah, I guess."

He sat up straight. "You got to loosen up, Matt. Ever since you got with her, she has you under her constant thumb. I almost miss Amanda, at least she let you be cool, ya know?"

I winced when he used Amanda's name. "Come on, Rebecca isn't that bad."

Brent looked away and laughed. "My wife doesn't harass me every second of the day, but then she's got the kids to attend to. Hey! That's what you need to do, is get Rebecca pregnant. Then she won't be bored. Yeah, yeah, that's it."

I stared at him, horrified. Two women with kids to deal with sounded like a personal hell. "Yeah, I'm not sure that's gonna work," I muttered.

But he had a point about Rebecca. When I was with Amanda she let me hang out with my buds without texting me unnecessarily every second. She wasn't insecure or needy. She gave me space and in return I gave her hers—a little too much, I'd realized lately. That made her that much more attractive. How I missed her for that.

"So what *is* up with you and Amanda?" As if he read my mind. "Separation can't be fun."

"No, it's not. We don't talk much anymore, besides, you know, about Joy." I looked away.

"Spit it out, man. You know you want to at least bang her on the side. It wouldn't be wrong. You two are married, after all."

I sighed and shook my head, mostly to hide that I'd had that thought myself a week ago. "Naw, that wouldn't work. She is capable of making life a living hell."

Brent shrugged. "If she was going to, she would have. Amanda was always cool like that. Hot headed, yeah, but she's a smart one when it comes down to it I remember."

Brent and his wife and Amanda and I used to hang out often. She just connected with people better where Rebecca was more of a homebody with just a small circle of close friends. I guess that was one thing I always liked about her. Rebecca balanced me out in that regard.

Without thinking, my phone, which I hadn't turned off even though I said I would, vibrated.

Why can't you watch the game at home? With me?

I frowned as Brent reached over and grabbed my phone. I tried to reach over, but he held it over my head. He typed something.

"There." He handed the phone back.

I read what he texted. *I just want to spend some times with the guys, so stop texting me, alright?*

I bounced my leg. "Shit, man. What the hell? She's going to be pissed!"

"Don't let her manipulate you. Boundaries, dude."

The football game began. "Weren't the others supposed to come?"

Brent asked for another beer. "Brody said he'd catch up

later. Says he had to drop his daughter off somewhere."

I sighed. "He was with his family, something I didn't have anymore. One daughter's dead and the other I get to be a part-time father to. It sucked. "

It was definitely time for something harder. I ordered myself a double rye on the rocks. Twirling around the glass, I watched the contents circulate.

I turned my attention to Brent who was focused on the game now. I was down in the dumps, and couldn't focus on anything but how shitty my life was.

"Touchdown." Brent bounced up from his chair. "Score! Come on, bring that defense, oh yeah!"

I stared down at my phone to yet another text from Rebecca. *Have fun. I just thought you'd want to spend some time, with you know, your girlfriend. But that's okay. Whatever.*

I shut off my phone finally. I wasn't in the mood for her pity party. I'd just tell her my phone died and was charging in the car.

Brent was peering at me. "She bitching some more?"

"Unfortunately. Hoping once the divorce is finished she'll lighten up."

"So what is the hold up?"

I exhaled noisily. "I'm just waiting a few months until Joy is over a year so I don't have to file for custody."

He sat back. "Is that all? Or are you having seconds thoughts? Man, it's okay. It's hard not to notice that you aren't over her."

"We're done." I had to keep reminding myself that Amanda asked for this divorce. I said at much.

"Well, yeah, I'm sure she didn't have much of a choice." Brent sat forward, his bottle between his legs. "I'm not suggesting, well, I kind of am, man, that you don't love Rebecca. But come on." He sat up straight. "You always look like you are walking on egg shells around that woman. At work, you are distracted and it's not secret even on my floor you're on a short leash."

"I'm distracted because I'm stressed out."

"Keep telling yourself that." He snickered.

"What the hell do you know?" I blurted, nearly wincing for how harsh it sounded.

"Because you used to talk so damn highly about your wife before shit hit the fan. But then, you became a pussy. Hate to say it, man. You don't talk like you love the damn woman. All your friends liked Amanda. You talked about her highly. If you were over your wife, and loved Rebecca you'd be divorced right now. No doubt about it."

I looked away. He was right, I was stalling. I was, for a moment, contemplating being with my wife again. I almost cheated on Rebecca with my wife, but I didn't go through with it. Jesus, what was wrong with me? With my life?

"Man, you're a fool. Least we can toast to that."

"Shut up!" My voice harshened. "Yeah, whatever."

Brent chuckled. "Chill man."

"Just drop it, okay?"

He leered toward me. "I'll drop it once you admit you love your wife. Just admit it."

"Fine, I still love Amanda." I said. "But she is with someone else, alright?" I lied. I just wanted him to drop the subject.

I ordered yet another double. Just the thought of yet another man enjoying my wife made me sick to my stomach. I didn't want her to move on. I didn't act on my feelings. I knew I had a responsibility to being faithful. But make no mistake, I still loved Amanda. It was so hard to shake these feelings. I just wanted to be rid of them – most days, anyway.

"Two to one." Brent said. He fortunately changed the subject. "What an idiot." He muttered at the screen. I was too preoccupied to even notice.

I forced myself to watch the game while Brent pulled out his phone and frowned at it. He texted furiously for a moment, then stood from the table. "Sorry, man, I got to run."

"Huh?" I asked.

"My daughter fell off the bed, banged her head up pretty good, and my wife is frantic, says she needs to go to the ER. Besides I'm sure Rebecca is waiting for you, huh?"

I waved him away with a fake smile. Brent finished off his drink and left.

He was going home to his family, to being a family man. Right now I wished I was him. I wished I had my family to take to the ER, however terrible that sounded.

I turned on my phone to a few missed calls from Rebecca and some frantic texts, demanding I text her back.

I simply texted her yet another lie. *Sorry my phone was dead. Why don't you come join me. My buddies left.*

I honestly didn't want her to come, but I didn't want to go home just yet. Maybe she'd be in a better mood, happy and we could have a good night. That was, if she agreed.

Fine. Text me the address.

I replied with the address and clicked out. Luckily, the bar was only a short commute. This was always the bar I liked to visit. It was Amanda and my favorite place, and it sort of just became a custom.

I ordered another drink and waited. My mind floundered, as I tried to think positively. Rebecca could pick up on my mood in a second, and if she sensed even an ounce of unhappiness she would instantly assume the worse. She would accuse me of thinking of my wife, which wouldn't be a lie, but she would dwell on it until I lost my mind.

I was so over it, honestly. I needed a break from Rebecca... The longer I lived with her, the more I remembered just how relieved I felt when I called it off.

The bartender handed me the beer and walked over to a small table in the mostly empty bar. Usually, it was busier than this, especially with a game on.

The game I ended up not even watching.

I kept glancing at the door, awaiting her arrival. My leg bounced under the table. A few minutes later, she arrived, changed into a black and white striped cocktail dress that framed her hour glass frame and sporting bright red lipstick. She looked stunning.

I smiled as I rose, walked over to her, and threw my arms around her. "I'm glad you came," I whispered in her ear.

A sweet scent of perfume radiated off her, and her breath smelled minty.

"You're not planning on having much more to drink are you?"

I backed up and my shoulders drooped. "Can't we just have a good night without your constant nitpicking?"

She frowned. "I just wish you weren't always drunk."

"I went to a bar. I'd love to just sit down with you,

enjoy your company and have a few drinks. You used to be so much fun." Under all this nagging, unjustifiable, unreasonable attitude she could be fun. We did have a long-term relationship way back then. I just wished she'd lighten up because she was just making me want my wife that much more.

She stood with her hands on her hip.

"I'll get you a drink," I asked. "What do you want?"

"I'll have a vodka and soda water."

I smiled, brushing my fingers along her jawline, forcing a meek smile from her. "Some things never change."

She shrugged. "Why change a good thing?"

She took a seat at the table where my nearly empty beer sat, as I slithered for the bar. The male bartender, now, was replaced by a female, who sported a similar look to Rebecca. She was skinny with long blonde hair and a piercing stare.

I fumbled my words but was able to get the order right. I was tipsy, and add in having a woman who's moods changed at the blink of an eye, I had to be careful. I returned to the table with the drink in hand and handed to her.

She beamed at me. "Thanks, babe."

"Anything for you." I finished off the last bit of my old beer before sipping another. "So how was your evening?"

"Sat around waiting for you. So what happened, did you friends ditch?"

"He had an emergency. Which worked out all right because hanging out with you is more exciting anyway." I smirked.

Deep down inside I wasn't particularly eager to see

her. Not that I didn't enjoy spending time with her, but lately she had been difficult. I just wanted her to be supportive and loving as before, not this insecure, constantly nagging girlfriend, who acted like we'd been married for fifty years. The bickering and shitty attitude just pissed me off. Some days I preferred being at work.

I glanced up at Rebecca. She twirled her hair around her finger. "Why do you always look so miserable?"

I shrugged. "I'm fine."

She rolled her eyes as she sipped her drink. "You are quiet."

I laughed, partly because I felt her reaction was ridiculous. "Since when is being quiet is a bad thing?"

Rebecca obviously didn't think it was amusing because her stare spoke volumes.

"Lighten up, Hun." I caressed her hand, which she tensed. "I'm just trying to think of a funny joke. I want you to laugh. You have a great smile." I realized how lame I sounded. The question was, did she believe it or was she thinking the worst like she usually did?

All of sudden she gasped and her face twisted. Before I had a chance to ask her what was wrong, she pulled me into a kiss. I pulled my hand behind her head, and pressed my lips against hers. When she naturally let go, she smiled. Beads of sweat dotted her forehead. "I love you."

"I-I love you too, babe." My mind scrambled. What was that? One second she was pissy and now she was all lovey-dovey. "What was that?"

She shrugged. "Nothing. Just wanted to kiss my sexy boyfriend," she said loudly.

I ran my hands through my hair. It felt like all eyes

were on us.

"Oh come on, don't get all red on me," she whispered.

I took a huge gulp of my drink. *I am not red! Ugh.*

She smiled. Something was on her mind. I just wished I knew what it was without actually asking. She'd get mad if I questioned why she was happy, like I was accusing her of having an ulterior motive.

"Do you have any change on you?" she asked.

"Yeah, why?"

She stood. "I just want to put on some music from that jukebox over there. You wouldn't mind would you?"

"Of course not." I reached in my pocket for my wallet and handed it to her. She took out a few coins and ambled over to the jukebox.

I sat there, sinking into the chair. My head felt heavy, like an immense weight was weighing me down. Maybe it was a mixture of too much to drink too fast, or something more, I couldn't put my finger on.

Crying by Roy Orbison, a strange favourite of Rebecca's played. Some side glances looked my way.

Rebecca returned to the table and sat with a mischevious smile on her face. She was up to something, but what? I picked up the beer bottle and chugged it.

I rose, stumbling to my feet. "I'm going to get another. Want anything?"

Rebecca reached for my hand that still rested on the table. "Wait."

I froze. "What?"

"Sit for a bit longer."

"I'll only be a minute."

I turned to head for the bar when I halted in my tracks.

Rebecca had me worried, but like usual, I just spaced out. I scanned the room without direction, seeing every brunette like Amanda, but not seeing them, not really. Some had dark hair like hers, some had her perfectly curved jawline, and some looked so much like her that I –

Wait, was that her? What was *she* doing here? Amanda?

I pushed my way over there, a little unbalanced, when a man in a suit, sat down with her.

The man handed her a pint.

Amanda smiled, as she sat close to the man, their legs nearly touching. She mumbled something I couldn't quite make out.

I turned to the bar and ordered two beverages. I made a side glance and Amanda didn't even bat an eye. She hadn't heard my voice. How couldn't she notice I was standing there?

I took the two drinks back to my own table.

Rebecca frowned. "Seriously? What took so long?"

I handed her the drink. "What? Did I get you the wrong drink?" Of course, that wasn't why she was mad but I was going to play dumb. I wasn't going to let on that I was thinking of my wife, with him. So, she was seeing someone. Already. So soon after what we did. Why would she? How could she move on so quickly?

I took a huge gulp of amber liquid. "Do you want to order some wings or something?" I suggested.

"No."

I rubbed my stomach. "Why not?" I knew I should leave but I didn't want to. I couldn't.

Rebecca rubbed the back of her neck, her face flushed.

"Just cut the crap. We both know she is here." She mumbled some colorful profanity under her breath.

"So what?" I said a little louder than I intended. "We were here first, so we will continue our night and not worry about her, okay?"

Rebecca was a little taken back. "Okay, I guess."

"So how about those wings?" I picked up the bottle and drank it before waving down a waitress. She hurried toward us, sliding between chairs too close and fans too loud.

"What can I get you tonight?" the beautiful brunette asked me.

"Some wings…honey garlic please," I said loudly, almost shouting. It was deliberate.

I glanced over the waitress at Amanda, who stared right this way. She bit her upper lip.

I smiled on the inside. Mission accomplished. The other man looked at us, too. He had a look of smug and surprise on his face, and I hated him. Every inch of him. How dare he dine with my wife. She shook her head before turning her attention back to her man. I swallowed hard as a lump formed in my throat.

"Seriously?" Rebecca's face was beet red now. Her fists clenched. "You are staring at her! Why?"

I shrugged. "I'm sorry." Only I wasn't sorry.

She stood straight up in her seat, her arms became rigid. "You're sorry, really? How do you explain staring at her?" She paused for a moment. "Well? Why don't you just leave and be with her already?"

"Shh! Sit down!" I whispered harshly. She rolled her eyes. "What happened to 'I love you, Rebecca.'" She paused and sat up straight. "Let's not forget about 'I'm over her, Hun. You're my life and I'm never going to leave you.' What a bunch of crap." She paced the table. Patrons were staring now, even Amanda.

"Calm down, Hun."

The bouncer, a large muscular guy who had at least fifty pounds on me approached the table. "Is there a problem?"

Rebecca sat down. "No, sir, there isn't..." She trailed off. "At least not at this table."

The man raised an eyebrow. "If he continues to bother you come find me."

Rebecca stood, grabbing her purse. "That's a good idea. Let's leave."

I sighed. I wasn't in the mood to go home. Not with my wife chatting it up with that other man. "You're free to go." I shrugged.

Brent's words rang in my head. Everyone liked Amanda better, and now I was starting to really understand why. I finished my drink, ignored Rebecca, who was trying to grab my hand to leave, and headed to the bar for another drink.

"Another, please."

The bouncer appeared behind me somehow and put a hand on my shoulder. "He's had enough," he told the bartender.

I looked at him, about to argue, when Amanda came up to the bar. "Can we get another pitcher?" She didn't even look at me. The bartender ignored me while I stood there, staring, speechless. The bouncer inched closer to me.

Amanda turned to me. "Go home, Matthew. You're

drunk." Her voice was soft, with a hint of concern. Just how she used to sound, and how she used to speak to me.

I hung my head in shame.

The bartender set a pitcher in front of her. I touched her shoulder, but she flinched. "Wait."

"I think it's time you left and stopped bothering this nice lady."

I tried to stand tall, but I stumbled into the bar, using my hand to stable myself. "She's my wife."

The bouncer towered over me. "Last warning, bud."

Amanda's date approached the bar, at least that's who I hoped it was. "Is there a problem, Amanda?" he asked.

I got a good look at the man, well, sort of. Everything was rather blurry now. A few inches taller than me, but I could take him. I couldn't take him. He couldn't have my wife.

Apparently, I might have said some of those things out loud.

"That's it, you're out, bud." The bouncer snatched me by the arm, squeezing painfully, and basically dragged me out of the bar. I struggled, but he shoved me outside and I tripped over my feet into the cement.

Rebecca ran out after me. "Stand up, you are acting like an idiot." Rebecca said as she held out her hand, but I shooed her away. She huffed as she turned, her back facing me. "I'm calling a cab."

I struggled to my feet, the cold air hitting me like a ton of bricks. Rebecca helped me to a bench. I slumped over, holding my face in my hands.

"What was that in there?"

I forced myself to make eye contact. "The bartender

wouldn't give me a refill."

She clenched her fist. "You know what I mean, with you and Amanda."

I glared at her. "Nothing." I wanted to tell her to fuck off and leave me alone. "She told me to go home. See, she doesn't even want to see me, either, so why are you being a bitch?"

Rebecca slapped me in the chest. "Go be with her, then." She stood with her hands on her hip. "Go into that bar, up to the table with her and her new boyfriend and be with her. You go be that desperate, drunk husband. See if she falls all over for you. You're pathetic, Matthew, you always were."

I stared at my blurry hands, my head swimming in beer and regrets, and everything around me slowed to a crawl. My thoughts spun around and around. Rebecca was right. Amanda was here with another man. That man was enjoying my wife. He was laughing with her, holding her, and probably later would be having sex with her.

It should be me.

"The cab's here."

She opened the door for me to get in. I moved over to let her in, but she slammed the door, and walked away. I guess she was leaving me to make my own way home.

14

For the rest of the evening, my phone pinged. I didn't bother to check my messages. Joy was in good hands with my mother, and if it was an emergency, she'd call. Matthew was the only one who would message me. As I expected after the Uber dropped me off at the house, I slinked into bed to check my messages and there were a half dozen texts from Matthew.

I slipped off my dress and into a comfy oversize sweater Matthew had left behind. After seeing him earlier that night, I felt a twinge of regret and longing for him that confused me. He was not himself, and it bothered me. I wasn't sure what that meant for me. I had been in limbo for months, dragging my feel, subconsciously hoping, I'm sure, for Matthew to come around. Then I invited him in because I wanted to know where we stood. I thought he was having seconds thoughts, then he rejected me. He was a confusing man. I crawled under the covers, and reached for my phone. I had one text from Hank.

I hope you had a good night, despite your drunk ex. Talk to you tomorrow.

It was a decent night, I supposed. I wished Mathew wasn't there and I wished I didn't have to witness him making a fool of himself. His drinking was out of control and I was worried about him. I thought the impending divorce would be good for him, but maybe it was taking a toll on him. But why? Every time I had seen him, except for the last few times, he seemed so happy. He smiled while Rebecca hung all over him. And when he wasn't happy it was after we talked about Ivory. He did move in with Rebecca the moment I asked for a divorce. I wondered if things weren't as rosy over there and he was having second thoughts.

I had a good time, I texted Hank. *I'll text you tomorrow.*

Hank didn't make the same impression as Matthew when we first met. Hank was a little more like your everyday Joe. Or maybe it was because I wasn't twenty-one but a mother with a child. The only thing I could say was Hank was fun, and polite.

I scrolled to the messages Matthew sent me, including the last one ten minutes ago.

Why won't you talk to me, Mandy?

I sighed. *You're drunk.*

I don't know why I even replied. I'd had a few drinks myself so maybe that was why.

A few minutes later he replied. Why, I don't know.

Why were you with that guy?

I found myself rolling my eyes. What did he expect? What did he honestly expect me to do? Stay single and miserable for the rest of my life? He didn't want me but also didn't want me to move on. Seriously? Worst of all, he acted on his drunken feelings in front of Rebecca. It'd just be another thing to add to the list of things she'd hate about me. It'd only make things more awkward during custody exchanges. Then, the anxiety crept up. She could go around spreading lies about me or, I pray, wouldn't take it out on Joy.

My thumb hovered over the touch screen for a moment, before I fired off: *If I knew you were there I wouldn't have gone there. I'm not trying to rub it in. I'm just having fun, which looks like you should have been doing.*

My heart sank a little. I should be jealous. I should be over the moon that he was having second thoughts. My friends and my mother all said he'd come crawling back, and I was righteous and thought he would, too. Now his true intentions, even if he was drunk, were screaming.

It's Roger all over again.

I bit my lip as I read his text. Ouch, that stung. He had to throw that in my face. He had to throw my mistake, my poor judgement back at me. I get that he was hurting, that he was jealous, but he had no right. He had no right to judge me. I sat there for a good few minutes typing and deleting a response. What I really should have done was not reply at all. He was emotional. I was emotional and we both had been drinking. We said things we didn't mean when we drank.

Instead I typed. *Let's talk tomorrow when we are both sober.*

I miss you.

Really? I sat there dumbfoundly.

It's true… But you went out with that other man.

My heart fluttered a bit. Did he actually miss me? Or was he trying to make me feel badly for having fun with another man.

I'm going to get some sleep. I think you should as well.

I set the phone on end table, turning it to silent, and turned to go to sleep. This conversation had gotten too personal, too emotional and it needed to, if it was needed at all, to be discussed sober.

***

The next morning, I woke up to a string of more missed texts from a drunken Matthew. He finally stopped after two hours of no response. I had picked up Joy from my mom's house and now was sitting down to relax. On the way home I got one final message.

I'm sorry about last night.

I stared at the text. At least he apologized and I could sense he felt embarrassed because he and everyone else in that bar saw him dragged out of the bar like an unruly drunk. It could have been so much worse. At least he got home safe.

You need to get a control on your drinking. It's not good for you or for Joy to see you like that.

I reached for the end table where I had stashed the divorce papers.

I flipped over on my stomach and stared at the papers he dropped off over a week ago. I had signed them, but was postponing giving them back to him to file. Though after seeing him sloshed at the bar, I realized just how much postponing this divorce was holding us both back. I picked up my phone. What I needed was a distraction and that distraction was Hank.

There's this little diner downtown we should check out. It may not seem like much, but they serve an amazing BLT. What do you think?

A small grin crossed my face. Despite our awkward first date, Hank really surprised me at the bar when my husband was making a fool of himself. It was so bloody obvious that Matthew was jealous, just like he had been when I hooked up with Roger. Yet he was the one who had moved in with another woman and turned me down again. Whenever I tried to move on, he fell apart and crumbled to the ground. He couldn't handle himself. Maybe it was a sign.

Hank's response was swift. *That sounds great. Maybe this week.*

Things with Hank were great so far. Running into him at the grocery store seemed like a blessing in disguise. I smiled more in the past few weeks than I had during the whole of last year. I even started dressing up more. I'd put in a conscious effort every morning to do my hair, put on makeup, and dress like an actual human.

At the same time, there was an immense weight on my heart. I couldn't stop thinking about Matthew. The constant memories housed by these four walls weighed on me. He was unraveling, drinking heavily, and deep down, I knew he was unhappy. I just didn't want to be a part of his train wreck. I wanted my husband, but not this version of him. Maybe the man I married was gone? With Hank, it was new, exciting, and a relief.

What are you doing tonight? Hank replied.

Joy and I are going to spend it at home, I guess.

Damn. That's disappointing, but hopefully sometime this week.

I'll let you know.

As much as I was tempted to go hang out with him, I had responsibilities that I needed to deal with. Earlier today, I started to look at rentals. Sure, it wouldn't be in this neighborhood, but with the money from the sale of the house, I could start over fresh in a new place with Joy.

I stood and paced around the room. I wanted to stay in

this house where Ivory was born and where the accident had taken place. This was the only house Joy had ever lived in. It was the house Matthew and I bought shortly after we got married. Since Matthew and I weren't a family anymore, it was time to find a new place with new memories.

Now that the pain of losing Ivory was wavering, reality had begun to unveil itself and show me that I was holding onto something that just wasn't there. I was holding on to a bad memory and it was holding both Matthew and I back.

I sat back on the bed and retrieved my phone. I texted Matthew.

I'm going to stop by and drop off these divorce papers. It's time.

I knew Rebecca blamed me for everything, probably including Matthew not getting over me, but that would change soon. If I sold the house and our divorce was finalized, there would be nothing left for her to blame on me. She'd be free to have him all to herself.

My phone buzzed and I snatched it up without thinking.

Okay.

Across the hall in the nursery, Joy woke from her nap. I could hear her giggling and babbling to herself. During the last few weeks, she had started to sleep for longer stretches at night and was pulling herself up on furniture. She was going to turn one in the next few weeks, and I had yet to discuss with her Dad how he wanted to split up the day.

I hadn't even planned a first birthday for her. With Ivory, we went all out. We invited all our friends and family. Matthew's mother spent so much money on gifts and decorations. After Ivory passed away, she couldn't be bothered. She probably only saw Joy maybe a dozen times since she was born and never more than a few hours. The pit in my stomach weighed me down. I'd be surprised if she even showed up at all. These days, I couldn't count on her for anything.

I picked up Joy and walked into the living room. I sat her on the floor, opened the newly installed baby gate, and walked into the kitchen to grab her a snack. Toast with butter was her thing. One would think she was starving by watching the speed at which she devoured it. She was just like her father in that regard. They both had big appetites. I buttered the bread after it popped out of the toaster, and handed it to Joy, who cooed with glee.

"Now, who's a hungry girl?"

"Ma, ma, ma, ma," she replied. She had been saying it technically for a few months now, but only recently that she was saying it in context.

I remember Matthew saying, during the few times we were able to have a decent conversation before I asked for a divorce, that her first word would be dada. I remembered thinking, cocky and all, that wasn't going to happen. I was mean and jaded, but I told him that she would say mama first. Now that it had happened, it made me feel a little sad.

Now that I thought about it, it was the little things I said that stacked up and left a lasting impression. Maybe we were so busy nitpicking and insulting one another that we damaged one another until we were full of resentment. After ten years of marriage we did know how to push each other's buttons, and it was unfortunate that we did it at a time where we were both vulnerable.

I glanced at Joy as the guilt crept up again. I had just spent some time away from her and I would have to find another babysitter when I went to talk and deliver the papers to Matthew.

It was going to be emotional. It was going to be hard. Only it had to be done, for both our sakes. I was going to start looking for rentals and into getting a more formal custody arrangement for Joy. We'd sell the house, split the debt and go our separate ways.

He did insist on a separation instead. He couldn't fool me. It was likely what the lawyer told him. It surely wasn't Rebecca telling him that. He couldn't fool me. He was trying to keep the peace on both sides. Well, I was relieving him from the duty.

I texted my mom asking if she would watch Joy for a few hours and explained why. She happily texted back, saying she was glad that I was finally getting myself out of limbo. Great, another shit sandwich I had to eat. My mother used to adore Matthew, and now she was furious with him. She would get quiet, antsy, and short whenever I brought him up or mentioned Joy going to see him.

We can go for ice cream afterward. My mom texted me. It was her way of saying she wanted to celebrate.

Maybe. I'm going to get changed.

Then I turned over to my conversation with to Matthew. *I'll be over there in a bit. I'll text you when I get there.*

I picked up Joy, changed her and got a bottle ready for her. I only ever pumped twice a day, for daycare.

"Ready to go to grandma's?" I asked her.

She squealed in agreement followed by a string of *mamama…*

"I'm so glad you are excited. I'm sure grandma will be as well.

I took the diaper bag and divorce papers and headed out to the car. I dropped Joy off at my mother's house before proceeding on the long drive to Matthew's.

I drove slowly and in total tranquility. This felt so right, and I knew I would be okay. I could move on.

I drove passed an apartment with a for rent sign. *Two bedroom suites, 1000.00 a month.* It was a bit of a stretch, but I thought I could come up with that, especially for the area it was in.

I drove down another street. I could picture myself living in any of these cute houses. I'd buy some new furniture, a new television and I'd make it my own. Maybe I'd have the courage to donate the rest of Ivory's clothing and toys. A new, fresh start was just what Joy and I needed.

I felt ready. As soon as I pulled up in front of the condo I texted Matthew. *I'm here.*

Then I waited.

A few minutes later, Matthew and Rebecca came from behind the gate onto the sidewalk, and I got out of the car. Rebecca stayed a few feet back, her hands on her hips and a frown on her face. She had a real nerve being all angry, when she was the one who stole my husband. Matthew walked up to me, shoulders slumped and a certain sadness radiating from him.

I swallowed hard as I handed him the divorce papers. "They are signed and ready to be filed."

Matthew's hand shook as he took them. He had an inward gaze, his lips pressed slightly. He let out a heavy sigh. "This is it?"

I nodded. "We have to stop dragging this on. I've decided I'm ready to sell the house, split the equity and move on." A tear threatened to emerge under my eyelid and I whisked it away. I was sad that it was coming to an end, but I couldn't live like this anymore. I didn't want to hurt anymore and I didn't want to watch Matthew hurt either.

He nodded slowly. "Thanks, I guess." He responded flaccidly.

"I'll talk to you later," I said.

"Amanda, wait."

He held the stack of papers close to his chest. "I-I don't know..." He paused and gaped at me.

Rebecca walked up beside him, her arms crossed, and her chest thrusted out, wearing a huge smile on her face "It's about time," she said in a condescending whisper. It was off-putting that she appeared to be enjoying all this. The sad thing was I don't think she realized just how conflicted Matthew was. I wasn't even sure he truly wanted her, but it wasn't my place to say anything.

"Have a good night, Matthew."

I turned to head back to my car. On the inside I was drowning. I never anticipated Rebecca, the woman my husband chose over me standing there. I was so confident on the way here, but now, reality hit home. It would be hard to let go of ten years together. So many memories erased, finalized by a simple signature at the bottom of a sheet of paper.

I fiddled to find my keys when Matthew grabbed my hand. "Wait."

I halted, turning to stare at him. "What?"

"Just wait, please."

I glanced behind him at Rebecca, who had daggers shooting from her eyes. I looked back at Matthew. "You should go be with your girlfriend."

"She can wait!" Matthew replied curtly.

I glanced downward.

Rebecca bounced from foot to foot, her fists clenched.

"Matt, you have things you should tend too. You need to go be with your girlfriend, especially after what happened last night."

Rebecca's nostrils flared and she looked about to blow.

Matthew shook his head and exhaled exasperatedly.

"I mean it. Last night you embarrassed me and you embarrassed Rebecca. I really think you need to go spend some time with her."

Matthew didn't move and continued to stare, the envelope still in hand. We stood there awkwardly, neither saying a word.

Rebecca marched closer to me. "Look, you dropped off the papers. About time, by the way. Why don't you just leave already?"

I took a step back, ignoring her. "Good night, Matthew. It seems like you have things to attend to."

Rebecca marched closer. "I'm so sick of you. I have kept my cool, but my patience is growing thin. You act all innocent. First you dump him, then he moves in with me. Then you start playing on his emotions, after you sleep with your boss. You are so unbelievable. I don't know. . .

Matthew put his hand on Rebecca's shoulder. "Calm down."

Rebecca frowned, the lines on her forehead became prominent. "Calm?" She glared at him then back at me. This was my cue to leave, but for some reason I didn't move. "Why don't you just go away? You're using your daughter as a tool to get close to Matthew, it's *so* obvious. Whenever he tries to move on, you'll do anything to make him second guess our relationship. You're like an evil witch trying to cast a spell on him!"

As much as I wanted to fight back, I sighed. "We're divorcing, so what more do you want? I'm not going to sit here and argue with you! You know what? He's all yours!"

Matthew tried to hush Rebecca but she pushed him away.

"Back off and stay in your place, if you know what is good for you!"

I took a step forward. "Is that a threat?"

Rebecca smirked. "It's a promise." She paused. "Matthew will soon realize what a mistake being with you was. He'll realize what a bad mother you are and he'll do whatever it takes to give Joy a better life. His ten-year nightmare will be over. Mark my words!"

It was one thing to be intimidated by me. I tried so hard to sympathize with her even after she slept with my husband. The way Matthew dumped her years ago for me was horrible. But now she crossed a boundary and there was no going back. How *dare* she bring Joy, and my motherhood, into this? That was something she'd never understand.

"He will dump you, like he dumped you before," I shouted.

Rebecca snickered. "Whose bed does he sleep in?

Hmm, Amanda? Who do you think he ran to when Ivory died? It sure as hell wasn't his wife! Why is that? Oh, because you were boning your boss!"

I winced, but didn't let her throw me off. "Oh, really? Did he tell you he kissed me and that we almost had sex?" I spit back just as quickly. "Or did he ever tell you why he dumped you in the first place?"

Matthew just stood there between us, looking at us both, horror marked on his face and his jaw hanging open. He covered his face in his hands. I did promise I wouldn't tell her, but she needed to get off her high horse. What good would Matthew's lies do for anyone?

Rebecca laughed. "You think you have me all figured out, but let me tell you, Mandy. He's with me. He chose me. He hired a lawyer to take Joy away from you. Did he tell you that? He may be taking a bit longer than usual to get over you, but in the end he chose me."

I bit my lip as an all familiar pain hit me in the gut. Matthew now stood behind Rebecca like a coward, but he even looked surprised. She had opened a can of worms, she would soon regret everything. I had kept my cool, despite wanting to unload on her so badly. For her to mention Ivory's name in such vain and to threaten me? Wow, she had another think coming.

"Nothing to say, bitch?" She jeered. "I'm not surprised, because you are nothing but a sad, pathetic, woman."

"Yeah, says the woman who got jilted just before her marriage." I said. "Did Matthew tell you he never wanted to marry you? That he was planning to leave you at the alter?" It was true. Matthew told me numerous times that proposing was a mistake. "Or how he would purposely get drunk just to enjoy sex with you?" I grinned. "He felt sorry for you. He was just too afraid to hurt you, until he met me. Remember the only reason he's living with you is because *I* asked for a divorce. Otherwise you'd still be his *sidepiece*. So good riddance to you, whore."

Rebecca put her hands on her hips, and calmly, coldly and calculated announced, "At least I didn't leave my daughter unsupervised to be hit by a car."

Without a word, she turned, strode past Matthew, and disappeared around the corner of the house.

Matthew and I glared at one another. He said nothing, his face flushed.

After a quiet, surreal moment I looked at him. "*You* chose *her*."

I turned and got into my car. That was the woman he chose over me, his wife. I was even more relieved to free myself from him and that train wreck.

15

I lounged by the pool, buying time until I found the courage to confront Rebecca or she forced contact with me. The signed stack of divorce paper lay beside me. I thought Amanda would have postponed it for a bit longer. But after tonight, after the brutal fight between those two, all chances of hope were slashed.

Call me when it's a good time to go over the final settlement agreement. We can list the house, split the equity, split the debt and the remaining assets and go our separate ways.

How did I find myself in this mess? Leaving my wife was supposed to make everything easier. Now she was with another man and I was with a woman who wouldn't stop bitching, nagging, and was starting to show her true colors. Rebecca never changed. She'd only gotten worse.

I tried to formulate a reply back to Amanda's text. Her sympathy waned and all that remained was pity. That was just the day, when a man's wife pities him. It was a kick to the ego, and I just didn't know what to about it.

A child about Ivory's age came to the poolside with her mother. I sucked in a breath and felt a heavy weight on my chest. I missed her so much. Life was so good. I had it all, a beautiful wife and a smart daughter. Then it was all taken away. What was even worse, here I was wanting my wife back.

Up on the top balcony of Rebecca's condo, I met her glare. I was a glutton for her abuse. The moment I walked through the doors I knew I would be in for an earful. I could almost rehearse word for word what she would say: *'Why don't you go be with her'* or *'She is such a bitch.'* This encounter would come out of nowhere, unprovoked, as usual. Amanda did the very thing Rebecca had been pressuring her to.

I stood up and made my way to the elevator. I might as well face the inevitable. I'd play it cool, sweet talk, and hopefully she wouldn't make the rest of my night a living hell or drive me to drink, which was probably what I'd end up doing anyway.

I paused outside the door to the condo. I could hear some rummaging, and Rebecca pacing. She was furious, and her loud footsteps gave it away. That and she was retaining her anger under the disguise of *keeping* busy.

I took a deep breath and let myself in.

Rebecca stood in the kitchen and clenched her jaw as she saw me enter. "About time you showed your face!"

I sighed. "I wanted to give you some time to calm down."

Her eyes narrowed. "Calm down?" She laughed sarcastically. "You want me to calm down, after your wife verbally attacked me?" She shook her head. "You are unbelievable!"

A lump formed in my throat. She just had no idea that she was the one who started it, and attacked Amanda unprovoked. I felt like such a coward for not stopping it before it got too out of hand.

She shook a fist while she glared with an intense, fevered stare.She clenched her jaw, her teeth grinding. "So don't tell me you are defending her, after everything she did? Seriously?"

I didn't want her to scream at me so I tried to reach out to hug her. Why I don't know, but she pushed me away.

I tried again. "I'm not defending her. I just don't want to be attacked." I walked over and dropped the divorce papers on the table. "She signed the papers. Now, it won't be long until the divorce is finalized. Then we can both be happy. Isn't that what you want?" Even as I said the last bit, it left a bitter taste in my mouth.

She bit her lip, her face beet red, perspiration dotting her forehead. "Yes."

It really was unfortunate for her that I was having serious second thoughts over the whole relationship. I just hoped her words to Amanda were because of the heat of the moment and because she was nasty. When she used my daughter's name in vain, she had used my daughter's accident as a mean to hurt my wife.

This time she tried to hug me. I didn't refuse, but my posture was stiff and unwelcoming. I pulled away after a few moments.

She sneered. "So..."

"What?"

"What she said, was it true?"

I looked at her confusedly. "What true?"

She rolled her eyes. "About needing to be drunk to have sex with me. That conversation."

I hesitated, but then quickly said. "I don't remember what I said back then." I forced myself to remain stone-faced. Everything Amanda said and much, much more was all true. I talked a lot of shit about Rebecca. I had forgotten just how relieved I felt when I left her. At the time, Amanda had been the escape I needed, but back then, I ended things with Rebecca before I went for it.

She paced back and forth. "So you did say it. If you didn't you would know."

"I said I don't remember, but I don't think I did, okay? Amanda was probably just mad. Ignore her."

Goosebumps formed on my arms and legs. I didn't like where this was going.

"That is why you need to go to court for custody and take Joy away from her. She is unstable, and will make up lies to make sure you don't get to see her at all."

Her comment took me by surprise, and I stood there speechless. She didn't seriously just say that, did she? What in the world was she thinking?

"See? You're lying to me." Spittle flew from her lips. "Why are you defending her? Why are you letting her get away with this? She came to our house, and called me a whore, and you stood there and said nothing!"

I open my mouth to defend myself, but she put one finger to my lip.

"Save the excuses."

What I really needed was a drink. More and more, I had been drinking just to deal with her tantrums. I knew it was starting to spiral out of control but I didn't know of any other way to deal with her. She was being unreasonable. She just didn't want to admit she was being a bitch. I was really over it.

"Answer me!" she shouted.

She was so unreasonable she didn't even realize she shut me down before I was able to answer anything.

I stood up. "I tried to, but you shut me down."

"What were you going to say? That you weren't

defending her? That I was in the wrong, and that I should let your wife, who you claim to be all over, treat me like shit, and I stand there and do nothing, right? That is what you want me to do. You don't want me to hurt the little snowflake's feelings."

I squared my shoulders and took a deep breath. "You both had a childish argument. Get over it. You are making a bigger deal out of this than it needs to be." In reality, the petty argument wouldn't have happened if Rebecca stayed inside, and let me get the signed divorce papers. Instead she just had to inject her damn self into something that had nothing to do with her.

She curled her lips. "So you are defending the woman who is responsible for your daughter dying. Got it." She paused. "Why don't you sleep on the couch tonight and figure out what it is you want."

"Fine!" I didn't want to sleep beside her anyway.

I felt relieved. She huffed and puffed and stormed to the bedroom and slammed the door. Well, good riddance to her. I sighed, and plopped on the couch, my head planted in my hands. What did I want, she had asked. I wanted to be rid of all this drama, all this bullshit I dragged myself into. My heart raced and I was so sick of walking on eggshells around her. The way she blamed Amanda for the idiot piece of crap who hit and killed my baby girl was heartless. Why did I bring her back into my life?

Soon the bedroom door opened, and Rebecca threw a pillow at me. "Here." Her voice dripped with scorn and ire. Little did she know that I was looking forward to sleeping on the couch and away from her.

She stood there, arms akimbo, waiting for a response

perhaps. Too bad. I wasn't going to give her one.

"Whatever," she mumbled as she turned to the bedroom.

I took the pillow and threw it beside me. When the bedroom door closed, I snuck quietly into the kitchen. I looked above the stove, and the half bottle of tequila was gone. I looked behind some pot and pans for the unopened bottle of wine Rebecca hid, but it too was gone. *God damn it,* I thought. *She must have thrown it out after last night.*

I contemplated going to the store to pick up more but stopped. She would know something was up if I tried to sneak out. She had amazing hearing and would hear me leave. I wouldn't hear the end of it. I sighed and slumped back on the couch. The springs under the microfiber were shot. Rebecca and I had talked about getting a new couch shortly after I moved in, but it never happened.

I grabbed my phone, which surprisingly Rebecca hadn't tried to snatch.

How about tomorrow morning, before lunch? I typed. *There was something else I wanted to talk to you about.* I texted Amanda.

A few minutes later the phone pinged again. *I work tomorrow. Afterward?*

I took a deep breath. *I am taking the day off tomorrow to do some errands. I'll have the daycare and mortgage payment in the account before tomorrow.*

In an earlier conversation, when Rebecca was really chirping in my ear, I said I was only going to pay half of her daycare expense. Now, I felt terrible. I wondered if she could even afford it. I'd always been the one who made more money, while she still worked in that shitty call center for minimum wage.

Okay. I'll text you after I'm done work tomorrow. Okay?

I sighed. *All right.*

If you are planning on taking the day off tomorrow, why don't you spend some time with Joy?

Tomorrow wasn't my day with Joy. I wished I could wake up, and go to sleep every night with my daughter in the same house as me. The pit in my stomach ached. I was missing out on so much of her life. I realized I really just wanted my wife back. I wanted my marriage back. But what could I do? Clearly, Amanda was moving on.

The last thing I needed was for Amanda and Rebecca to go at it again. *I'll stop by the house tomorrow morning to pick her up.*

Sounds good.

Amanda sounded so business-like. I wanted so badly to ask her how she was doing. How she was feeling? I wanted her to ask me how I was doing. I wanted her to say what a bitch Rebecca was, but instead she said nothing. Was she not thinking of me like that?

I lay down and closed my eyes, only I couldn't sleep. There was a pounding in my ears. I didn't know what to do. I had promised Rebecca I'd do well by her, that I wouldn't hurt her again. But deep down inside I made a mistake. My marriage was in trouble and she was there for me at my lowest, but now, her true intentions were obvious. I missed my wife. I missed my daughter. I wanted my family back.

***

The next morning, I woke at 5:30 a.m., earlier than I usually did. First things first, I called in sick. I lied, saying I had a migraine. My life was one big migraine, so maybe I wasn't lying, but stretching the truth.

I brewed a pot of coffee and sat heavily at the table. Any minute, Rebecca would be up. She usually woke up before me if I chose to sleep in and skip breakfast. I used to wake up with her to keep her company, but of late, I hadn't. I used any excuse I could to avoid her. She would be surprised this morning that I was awake, or maybe not. She knew the couch was uncomfortable, which was probably why she kicked me out of the bed in the first place.

After I poured myself a cup of coffee she entered the kitchen in a robe.

"Oh, you made coffee?" she asked.

"Yeah, help yourself." I replied as I looked away.

She poured herself a cup and sat at the table beside me.

"You're up early?"

What was Rebecca's agenda? Last night she was pissed and this morning it was business as usual?

I nodded. "I'm going to go in and catch up on some paperwork." I lied.

"Can't Susan handle that?"

"No."

"What are you doing at lunch? Maybe we can catch a quick lunch, spend some time together?"

I looked at Rebecca and faked a smile. "I'm busy, all right?"

Rebecca's smile drooped. She slouched her shoulders. She was disappointed. I didn't have the heart to tell her the truth. I didn't want to spend time with her. Right now I was trying to figure out my own life. I was going over to see Joy and hopefully talk about what happened last night. I was more concerned about how Amanda felt anyway.

"I'm sorry for making you sleep on the couch," she finally said. "It was lonely without you in bed."

Besides a sore back, it was pleasant for me not to deal with her nagging. I shrugged. "It's fine."

"How about we go out tonight? We won't talk about anything but us. Maybe plan that trip we talked about? What do you think?"

I sighed, my stomach in knots. "Let's see what time I get off. I don't want to promise anything. I don't want to make promises I might not be able to keep." I looked down.

She leaned over and kissed me on the forehead. "All right. I got to get ready for work."

I took a sip. "I'm going to go get dressed for work, here soon, too."

She left to go get dressed. I realized she never made any comment about last night. Maybe she knew she was in the wrong and didn't want to admit it or she just didn't care. I don't know why I even cared.

I slipped into the bedroom to grab my suit. I had to cover my bases. Rebecca was in the bathroom, buttoning up a baby blue blouse.

I hurried and got dressed myself, to avoid much unnecessary conversation with her. She made small chit chat and I responded in short answers.

I grabbed my briefcase.

"Have a good day," she said.

"You too, Hun." That word stung, as I turned away from her. It felt so wrong. "I'll talk to you later."

I walked out to my car, took off my suit jacket, and untucked my dress shirt. I took a deep breath as I drove away.

It was 6:15 when I pulled onto the street. The front door was open when I arrived. I entered the house. Amanda was dressed in a form fitting black dress and heels. Her hair was done, and she had make-up on. She looked put together. Ever since she was with that man, she looked great. She looked like the wife I remembered.

"I thought you had the day off," she said.

I exhaled noisily. "I didn't want Rebecca to know." I paused. "I'm sorry about last night."

Amanda shrugged. "Don't be."

"No, I really am. I didn't think she'd bring up Ivory." I lowered my head in shame. "I didn't realize she had so much anger."

Her arms hung limply at her sides as she stared at me blankly. "Soon our divorce will be done." Amanda yawned. "And after we put the house on the market, then we really won't have much need to communicate except dealing with Joy. It'll be easier for the both of us."

I shifted from foot to foot. "About that?"

"What else is there to discuss?"

"I don't want to be with her… With Rebecca." My voice was low. I had been thinking it, feeling it, and trying to compartmentalize it but it was a load off my shoulders to just say it. "I just can't do it anymore." I didn't look at Amanda. I wasn't even sure I was talking to her versus just at her. "I regret it. I regret her." I felt myself shrink. It was kick to the gut.

"You don't have to stay with her," Amanda responded. She walked up to me and placed her hand on my trembling shoulder. "Life is too short."

"I know." I waited for a moment, hoping she would offer for me to come back home, to our house. I could just come home, but it didn't feel right to just move back without her blessing.

Amanda leaned against the door. "It's none of my business, so I'm going to ask anyway, but why did you take the day off?"

I gaped at her, not sure what to say. I wanted to, but I didn't. I wanted her to ask me how I felt. I wanted to know if she still cared.

"What is on your mind?" Amanda asked as she came over to me and put her hands on my hips. "I know you well enough to know that there is something you want. So just come out and tell me."

"Can I come home?" I said. "At least until the *divorce* is final?"

Amanda looked shocked.

I felt like a piece of shit.

"Sorry, for asking." I sighed. "I'll just go rent an apartment or something."

Amanda shook her head. "No, don't go rent an apartment. I never said you couldn't come back home."

I small grin crossed my face.

"Really? You mean it?."

Amanda reached for my head but pulled away and checked the time. "I should get to work."

"Have a good day." I said as she slid past me.

"So does this mean for sure you're moving back?"

"Yeah, I didn't bring a lot of things over there, so I could be moved out before she gets off work."

Amanda bit her lip. "Maybe drop Joy off at daycare, and I can have my mom pick her up."

I looked at her funny. "Why?"

"We both know she is going to freak if she comes home to an empty condo. Do you really want Joy here in case she comes here looking for you?"

I glanced downward. "No."

She grabbed her keys. "There are a few ounces of breast milk in the fridge and formula in the cupboard."

"Okay!"

"Oh, and there is the spare key in the cupboard in the kitchen."

I walked into hallway, past the bathroom to the bedroom. The same grey comforter lay on our, her, I reminded myself, bed. In the room adjacent to the master bedroom was Joy's room. It used to be Ivory's bedroom before we moved hers across from the bathroom. Neither Amanda nor I could bear to open up her room. Soon we would have no choice. Soon we'd have to go through her stuff. That time was coming quickly with an upcoming move in the horizon.

I walked into the bedroom where Joy was staring at the mobile. She laughed when she saw me. I picked her up. "Hello, baby girl."

I felt like Joy had gotten so big, even though I just saw her a few days ago. It felt like I missed so much time with her. Now that I was moving back in temporarily, I'd get to spend a little more time with her.

"I'd love to spend the whole day with you, but Daddy needs to move his stuff back in." I walked with her out of the room, while not breaking eye contact. "Now I get to come home every day and see you. I hope, in time, maybe your mom and I can reconcile. It's been a tough year for all of us."

Joy just grinned, four teeth showing. Two on the bottom and two on the top.

"Thanks for listening, baby girl."

I held Joy to my chest and she babbled happily in her baby voice. She was such a daddy's girl like Ivory was. I made a promise to myself that I would make it up to Joy and be the attentive father I should have been the first year of her life.

I changed her and got her dressed before dropping her off at daycare.

My heart beat fast as I drove back to the condo. Rebecca wasn't going to take this well. She was going to flip out, and I didn't look forward to it. If she wasn't so unpredictable I would break it off with her in person instead of taking the coward's way out. Even Amanda was worried about her reaction, hence having my mother-in-law picking Joy up. My mother-in-law's reaction to me moving back into the house was another I wasn't looking forward to.

Inside the condo, I packed my stuff in boxes as quickly as I could. One by one, I loaded them in my SUV. I hoped none of the neighbors took notice and tipped her off. Worse yet, I hoped Brock and Marge, her parents, didn't show up unannounced. I shook Brock's hand and promised man to man I wouldn't hurt his daughter again. Here I was again, doing just that.

I reached into the closet where I had put the box of things Amanda took over the one day. The flap was open, and inside the box the things were rearranged and on top was my wedding band. Rebecca must have seen it. It could explain one of the many freak outs she had.

I closed the box and took it out. I hoped I didn't need to make a second trip. I wanted to be done with this place.

Just before noon, I placed my last box into my SUV. I took the condo key off my keychain and placed it on the kitchen table. I tidied up a bit, and did one last walk through to make sure I didn't miss anything. I locked the door behind me.

Inside the car, I checked my messages. I hadn't bothered to check them since the morning when I left for Amanda's.

There was a message from Rebecca from an hour ago. *How is work?*

I gulped and took a deep breath. *Just got out of a meeting.*

Before I could put my phone down, she responded. *Really? I drove by your office and your vehicle isn't here.*

I wiped at my forehead. I couldn't go back to Amanda's house yet, because that'd be the next place she'd look if she didn't come home first. How could I respond?

I ran out for coffee for the office.

I threw the phone on the passenger seat and drove away from the curb. What should I do? What could I do? I didn't expect her to go to my work. She never drove by my work. Or maybe she did and I just don't notice. I drove around, thinking of how I was going to break it to Rebecca.

I couldn't let her find out like that. I didn't know what I was thinking.

I pulled into the parking lot of the local supermarket. Maybe some booze would make the decision easier. I walked up and down the aisles until I reached the area where the hard liquor was. I grabbed a bottle of tequila and headed back toward the till where I froze, when I realized what I was doing.

I couldn't go back to the house with this. I wasn't going back to the condo. I was going home, back to my house, where my wife and daughter were. I vowed never to be drunk around my daughter. Amanda would surely kick me out and I wanted her back.

I paced a bit before I decided to put it back on the shelf. Instead I grabbed a soda. I never did like going into a store, wandering around, and not buy something. It was always a quirk Amanda found odd.

I sat back in my car, where I left my cell. *Angela said you didn't come in today. What is going on?*

Ugh. The cat was out of the bag. I realized I had two options. I could lie or I could be honest. *Fine, I didn't go to work today…*

I sent before I started to formulate another response. *I'm sorry, Rebecca.*

What else could I say? I began to text about how I wasn't feeling well, but then deleted the text. Then I began to type how I was going to spend some time in a hotel but stopped.

Then I typed another message. As my thumb hovered over the send arrow, I accidently sent that text before I could finish a complete thought.

Sorry about what? You know I hate lying. Where are you, sucking up to Amanda again?

There was the bitch coming out again. *I can't do this anymore.*

Do what?

I paused for a minute, before responding. *I was planning on telling you this in person, but decided it was best I didn't. I just don't think we will work out in the long run. You obviously aren't over how I broke off our engagement and got with my wife. That isn't her fault. It was mine. For Joy's sake, and for my sake, I just don't see a future. I need to focus on my impending divorce. I moved my things into storage. But I will deposit my half of the bills for this month into your account. I hope in time you realize this was for the best.*

There was no going back now. I didn't bother to drive away because I knew a response was coming. Instead of a text she called me. At first I debated letting it go to voicemail, but if there was ever a time where I deserved to feel her wrath it was right now. So I answered the phone.

"Hello?" I whispered.

"What the fuck?" She shrieked in my ear. "What do you mean you moved out? Answer me. Answer me right now! What is the meaning of this. Is this some kind of joke?"

"No?"

"It's her. It's that fucking bitch. She put you up to this! I should have known she would interfere. Oh my god, I tell you. She has what is coming to her."

"I know you are upset."

"You think? Are you dumb or something?"

"I made this decision on my own. I thought you

deserved an explanation but if you don't want to hear it, I think it's best to leave things here."

"Damn you," she screamed before she hanging up on me.

That was my answer.

16

Matthew sat at the kitchen table the following morning. He wore just his boxers and oversize slippers. Last night we had cuddled, and he slept like a baby. My heart skipped a bit. It was so obstinate. Last night, I had Matthew park in the garage out back, and I took the driveway, because as I expected, Rebecca's car drove by a few times. One moment, I caught her glaring at my house. It left me feeling uneasy. Joy spent the night with Grandma last night, but I knew, sooner or later, Rebecca would find out Matthew was here, and I had to be prepared for that, and I didn't feel the need to shelter Joy from that.

"Do you want any coffee?" Matthew asked. "I made a fresh pot." One of the things I had missed was Matthew always had fresh coffee brewed every morning.

I smiled and grabbed myself a cup. "Thanks."

I sat at the table with my phone. I had a few missed texts from Hank. I had been ignoring him since I had allowed Matthew to move back in.

Is everything all right? Hank texted.

I bit my lip and looked up at Matthew, who stared off into the living room. As long as he didn't ask me who I was texting. I didn't want to make this temporary situation even more awkward.

Yeah, just had a long day yesterday. And looks like I'll have another today. So might not text much.

My heart skipped in an unfamiliar beat. I was sorta dating Hank, but now that was up in the air with my husband back here. We were separated, but now we weren't. I didn't even know what to call us. We were divorcing, and about to list our house. But now he was here, and there hadn't been a single mention of what we were going to do.

Matthew turned to look at me. "Do you want me to take Joy to daycare?"

I nodded. "Okay, that'd be great." At least with Matthew here I didn't have to rush in the mornings and Joy could sleep in a bit more. I could take my time getting mobile in the morning before work. At least there was the bonus of having him around. That and I no longer looked at him with such disdain.

Matthew's leg bounced under the table. His face flushed.

"Are you all right?' I asked. But knowing him, his mind was in overdrive. "It's okay if you don't want to talk about it."

"I-I…" he mumbled, but his voice trailed off.

I reached over and caressed his hand. He flinched but made eye contact with me. "Are you worried about running into Rebecca?"

He frowned. "Kinda, yeah." He inhaled. "I was thinking about you."

The hair on the back of my neck stood right up. "What about me?" I hoped it wasn't what I thought it was. I didn't want to be a rebound because his relationship with Rebecca didn't work out.

"I missed you."

I turned away. "Me too." But then I remember the night I invited him in. The night he delivered the divorce papers, and the night he told me to move on. "But you rejected me." I recognized the strong disdain in my voice. I felt sad. A sudden hollowness in my chest.

"It was a mistake."

Matthew looked like he'd seen a ghost.

I looked at the time. It was almost time for me to start work. "I got to get going. We'll talk about this later." In reality, I had a few minutes to spare, but I needed to retreat. I couldn't deal with him right now. My throat burned. Did he really miss me, or did he just need me to fill some kind of void or to repair is ego?

I pulled out of the driveway. As I pulled onto the main street, Rebecca's car drove past me and down my street. I wanted to turn around and confront her, but I didn't. This wasn't my battle to fight. I gnawed on my upper lip. I couldn't keep my mind off the whole situation.

Matthew and I spent ten years together. He didn't just wake up one day and decide he didn't love me anymore. Our daughter died. Our marriage died shortly after. Maybe after some time apart, we both came to terms with things, and maybe we could save our marriage.

Then I remembered Hank. We barely knew one another, but he was new. He made me smile and it was so nice to get out and be desired again. Then there was Matthew. I wasn't the same size-two girl he met. Two pregnancies and fifty pounds later, I wasn't thin. I had the mom pooch and stretch marks. I had learned to accept it and embrace it these last couple weeks. Would I be able to maintain it, if I entertained reconciliation?

I pulled up to the parking lot. It was seven fifty. I still had ten minutes until I started. On the drive here I had got a few texts. A few from Hank and one from Matthew. I stood and stared. I wanted to check Hank's message, but I was drawn to Matthew. He was still my husband after all.

Have a good day, Mandy. There was a flutter in my chest. Matthew really did have a way to make it jump. I just hoped his intentions were genuine. I pondered for a moment to think of a response, but instead I just replied *you too.*

***

Five rolled around and I left not a minute later. Roger stopped me at the entrance and grinned. "I see you are looking a little distracted today."

"Unless there is something work related you need to discuss, I'm leaving."

He laughed. "Have a good day, *Mandy.*"

I gagged on my way to the car. For the longevity of the affair I found some comfort in him calling me that, but now it disgusted me. Matthew was the only one who called me that and didn't expect a damn thing in return. He loved me.

I was halfway to the daycare when my phone rang. I pulled over and answered it.

"Hello?"

"I already picked up Joy from daycare. I was thinking maybe we could grab supper and talk?"

I hesitated before agreeing.

"Okay, text me where you want to go. I'm just about to drive away from the daycare."

After I got off the phone, I texted him the address for a

local diner a few blocks from the house. I parked the car, and headed for the door. By the front door, Matthew stood with Joy. He reached over and pecked me on the cheek. I smiled and kissed him back.

Matthew, Joy, and I walked inside. Matthew went up to the counter and ordered us some drinks, while I settled Joy in the high chair. Reaching in the diaper bag, I handed her a teether. She had another set of teeth coming in. I thought for sure, with her birthday coming up, she'd have more than she did now.

When Matthew sat down, I looked at him. "What do you want to do for Joy's birthday?"

Matthew frowned. "I haven't thought of it."

I shrugged. "I haven't either until recently, but we still have time."

He sat there, fiddling with the cuff of his collar. "How about an intimate birthday party?"

I thought for a minute, and guilt washed over me. We didn't have an intimate party for Ivory. We had a grand party. It felt cheap and unfair to not do the same for Joy.

Matthew reached over for my hand. "I know what you're thinking."

"What?"

"Ivory had a big party, and you always imagined the same for Joy. It was all you talked about leading up to that day."

I nodded. "Yeah, I did."

"I just think, and I know my opinion doesn't matter, but…"

"It does, it matters to me. What do you think?"

"I just feel like we haven't' been there for Joy the way

we should have. We were separated, grieving, and I just feel like…" He paused. "I just feel like celebrating with her would be good for all of us. And…" He trailed off.

"And what?" I asked.

He rubbed the back of his neck and swallowed hard. "I just don't think your Mom and Dad will be too keen to see me. And my mom just couldn't be bothered these days, you know."

He was right. My mom was furious and made no secret she felt so much betrayal from Matthew. She wouldn't easily, if ever, forgive him. That was another obstacle, I wasn't sure I was ready to face. Mom's opinion of him was important to me. She was my backbone during this whole time, but would she understand if I gave Matthew and I another go?

"I'm sorry." He mumbled.

"Let's just stop apologizing."

I was sick of saying sorry and I just wanted us both to forgive.

I took a deep breath. "We spent so much time blaming each other for what happened to Ivory. We both hurt one another, because we didn't know how to cope. We didn't know how to support one another. We both sought comfort in other people. I just want to forgive, you know." I wasn't sure where I was going with this, but I had a lot of time to reflect on it. I spent the better part of four months, accepting things as they were.

A tear formed in Matthew's eye. For a man that rarely cried, he was moved by something. I grabbed a tissue and handed it to him. Flutters emerged in my chest.

"Then why don't we try again? For real." Matthew

suggested. "Nothing we do can bring back Ivory, but that doesn't mean her death signals the end."

So many thoughts circled in my head. I looked over at Joy who was slobbering and stringing together sounds that resembled what could be words. I always wanted my kids to grow up in an intact family. I still loved Matthew. I still thought about him every day, and now he was back in our house. We weren't divorced yet. There were so many factors. He was asking me. It wasn't me begging this time. It was him.

"What do you say?" he asked. Hope brimmed from his eyes.

"Okay," I blurted. Then I thought about Hank. He had been so nice to me, supportive and all. What would I tell him?

"What's wrong?" Matthew asked. "You don't seem too excited?"

I sighed. "I am. It's just a lot to take in."

Here I was opening up my heart again to him. I was letting him in. But there was still one thing I needed to discuss with him.

Matthew finished his cup of coffee. "Do you want to go home and celebrate with something stronger?"

"Actually, Matthew, there is something I want to discuss with you. Especially if we want to try and work on our marriage."

"Oh? What's that?"

"Your drinking." I said curtly. "I noticed you have been drinking a lot over the past couple months. I'm not going to dwell on the other night at the bar, or the few times I've seen you go into a bar, but I am concerned."

Matthew lowered his head. "I'll stop."

"Promise?"

"Promise. I don't want to lose my family a second time."

I accepted his answer but in the back of my head, I wasn't one hundred percent sure we would be able to reconcile. There was so much doubt in my heart, but I was optimistic. I had to be.

"Excuse me, I have to go to the bathroom."

I rose from my seat and scurried past the table to the lady's room. My mind was floundering. What do I tell Hank? I had been distant the past day, and he had to be wondering what was going on. We were planning another date, but here I was giving my husband another chance.

I sat inside the stall on the toilet seat and stared at Hank's number. He had been so sweet, and he made me come out of this ongoing funk I had been in. I started to live again, dressed up again and started to feel human again. I felt like I was deceiving him by giving him the impression I was not getting back with my husband.

I swallowed hard. I began to type a response but deleted it. I couldn't tell him I was getting back with my husband. That would make me sound selfish, but it was the truth.

The bathroom door swung open and I jumped. I really needed to just send the message before Matthew got suspicious.

I'm sorry I have been distant. I just think that I'm not ready to date right now. I hope you understand.

I sent the message and closed out of my phone.

When I exited the bathroom, Matthew and Joy were

standing outside the door. I followed him out to his SUV. He put her in her car seat.

"See you at home?" I said.

Matthew embraced me. This was really happening.

17

Amanda and I sat on the couch a foot apart.

"Are you alright?" I asked her. Today, she was quiet. Last night she tossed and turned. When I finally fell asleep, she must have moved into Joy's room and slept on the day bed.

Amanda stared at me. "I'm fine."

"It's just, you were in the other room…"

Amanda smiled weakly and placed her hand on my thigh. "I couldn't sleep. I just didn't want to wake you."

I glanced downward. Was it because of me that she couldn't sleep? All night long, I was thinking a lot. In two days, I had gone from being with one woman to another. Amanda was coming out of her shell, opening up to me. Deep down inside, I wondered if she was just agreeing because she felt sorry for me.

"It's just been hard, Matt," she finally said, "not with you, but with just everything in general."

I glanced at her trying to formulate a response. My goal was to reunite the spark, but it was hard. I didn't want to say the wrong thing and cause her to change her mind or remind her or myself of why we were in this situation in the first place.

A tear formed in her eye. "I just remember standing over there, and you laying here and how I said I wanted a divorce." She paused to wipe away the tear. "Like how we got to that point. How much we had drifted apart, and how bitter we were toward one another. It's just hard to think about that, and to think about how close we were."

Whoa, that was dark, I thought. Well, it had been the darkest day of my life. I remembered how much, at that point, I didn't even care. I immediately threw my wife away and didn't fight for her and ran straight for Rebecca. I left her to fend for herself, and I let her run to another man.

Amanda took a deep breath, almost choking. "Neither of us fought for our marriage." She hugged her legs, and stared at the wall. There was that barrier again, that sadness radiating from her.

I pulled her into my arms and we sat there in silence. It was symbolic. Only I wished I could read her, find out how she felt, and what I could do to make her happy.

"I have to go pick up some outfits my mom bought Joy. Then, maybe we can figure out what we want to do for Joy's birthday."

"Oh?" I asked.

"I promised her I'd pick them up yesterday. I've been postponing it and she is going to be getting suspicious. Do you really want her showing up here?"

I shook my head. My mother in law was going to flip when she saw me. Like I was Rebecca, I was already avoiding her. That woman wasn't someone you wanted to cross.

Amanda leaned over and kissed me. "I won't be long."

"I'll hold you to that."

Amanda grinned, as she headed for the door. "Joy should be awake soon."

I sat in silence as the front door shut. Careful not to wake Joy, I slithered into the kitchen. I had an urge to pour myself a drink. Today, there was an emergency water main break, and Amanda happened to have some paid vacation she hadn't taken, so we both had the day off, and yet all I wanted to do, or at least subconsciously, was pour myself a drink. I never realized how much my drinking had taken off since I got with Rebecca. It was ingrained in me. When I was in the presence of Amanda, the urge wasn't there.

I opened the fridge and grabbed a soda. I needed to fight these urges and if that became too unbearable, I could attend some AA meetings. What could I do to de-stress? I cracked open the can and sat at the oak table. Underneath the table was a cracked ceramic tile. I remembered that happened when Ivory dropped a toy on it, and I was so mad at her. We had just retiled the floor. My heart rattled. Even though she was such a perfect child, well both my daughters were perfect, she had still been a child.

I took a sip of the half empty can, and left it there on the table. I wandered down the hallway aimlessly and stopped at Ivory's bedroom door. All my senses seemed to stop when my hand went to her door knob. It had been a while since I had entered this room.

Three of the four walls were painted a baby pink, with the headboard of her bed facing a bright, hot pink wall. A few weeks before the accident, I had renovated this room. Ivory helped pick out the colors, and we had gone out and bought her a new bed. She had graduated from her toddler bed and she was so excited. She told us we needed to keep the toddler bed for the baby. On her little, matching desk by the window sat an untouched sketchbook. On the last page was a half-drawn picture of three stick figures.

Ivory was just beginning to form letters. She wasn't even four yet, but she was so smart, so inquisitive. I sat on her little wooden chair for the first time in over a year. I switched to the first page, and turned the pages of her sketch book, starting from the first page. I kept scrolling until I stopped at a picture of two figures. In big black lettering it said "Dady and Me." It made me jump, misspelling and all. I carefully tore the page out of the sketch book. I wasn't sure what I was going to do with it yet, but I felt the urge to take it with me.

I had always pictured how I'd walk her down the aisle at her wedding, and how Amanda and I would sit in the audience as she walked across stage to get her diploma. The reality struck, that was never going to happen. I'd never be able to get any of those memories with her. I stared down at Ivory's drawing. It represented how she viewed me and her. She made us both happy, and that was how I wanted to remember her. I wanted to remember her as the happy child she was.

I placed the sketch book back on her desk, and turned back to the page she had left it on. That should have been my cue to leave the room, but I didn't. Maybe it was time to face it. Face the fact that Ivory was no longer with us. A part of me felt like I was trying to pretend she didn't exist.

But I felt like holding on to this room, and all her stuff was just holding us back from grieving. It wasn't being used, and this room could be better used in another way. I was in great need of an at-home office. It was used as that before we found out we were pregnant with Joy, but we needed a third bedroom, so I gave it up. Maybe it was time to changed it back to its former function. I had considered when we did paint it to turn into Ivory's room, about eventually selling the house for something bigger.

"Matthew?"

I jumped and turned. I hadn't seen Amanda come home. She held a few hangers with a few cute dresses. "Those are cute," I mumbled.

Amanda stood stone-faced, her mouth slightly opened. She didn't say anything.

I turned and walked up to her and wrapped my arms around her. She didn't need to say anything, her body trembled, and it was evident, at least to me, that she was holding back the tears.

"What are you doing in here?" she finally asked.

I released her and glanced at her. "It felt like it was time."

She hung the hangers on the outside doorknob as she entered the room. "Pink was her favorite color, wasn't it?"

I smiled. "Yeah, it was. If we had let her, she would have dyed her hair pink as well."

Amanda waked over to the closet and opened it. She ran her arms along the neatly hanging outfits. "She dressed better than we did, Matt." She pulled a polka dotted summer dress from the closest. "For her first day of school." She ran her fingers alongside the hem. Amanda was always fussy about hems, and always wanted to buy the best quality.

There was as sense of stillness in the room. It wouldn't last, but it was what it was, for the moment at least.

Amanda placed the dress on the bed, and started pulling out outfits by the hangers and setting them on a pile.

"What are you doing?" I asked.

She returned to the closest to retrieve the last of the hangers. I had inkling of what she was doing but I wanted to know her thought process. What was going through her mind?

A slight smile formed on Amanda's face. "Like you said, it's time." She turned her gaze to the pile of Ivory's clothing. "They are just collecting dust, when there are so many other children who could benefit from them. I was thinking, maybe we could donate them to a children's home. Think of all the children in need who could benefit from her clothes."

I stood there for a moment and thought about it. Usually we sold the girls' old clothing to recoup some of the money we spent on buying them. Amanda wanted to give them away, and obviously she had put a lot of thought into it, so I nodded. "If that's what you want to do."

She frowned. "Do you think it's a bad idea?"

I was taken aback. "No, not at all. If you want to do it, I support it."

Amanda circled the room. "I just feel like someone less fortunate than us could find joy out of Ivory's stuff. It just doesn't feel right profiting off her *death*. I had been thinking about it for a while. I just never had the courage or strength to do it. I want someone else to experience and appreciate her stuff. I just think that is what she'd want. Right?"

Amanda's explanation made sense.

"Okay, let's do it."

We were both in that mindset, and if we didn't make a decision on what to do with her things, we'd continue to self-wallow over what to do. After all, her passing almost destroyed us, not just as individuals, but our marriage as well.

Amanda picked up the hangers and plopped them in

my arms. "Can you take them into the living room?"

I did as she requested and took the clothes and laid them on the coffee table.

Back in the room, Amanda stood and stared at a blank wall. She didn't even turn to meet my gaze when I walked in. "I can't believe it's been a year. The actual anniversary was last month, and I had been keeping myself so busy, that it went by without a second thought."

I didn't say anything. On the one-year anniversary of her death, I spent the entire day at the bar getting drunk, then I went home and drank some more until I passed out. It wasn't a very productive day, but that day was never going to be great again, no matter what.

"Do you ever think about that day?" she asked.

"Almost every day," I said. I wished she hadn't brought it up, but how could she not when we were standing inside her bedroom, with the reminder of her screaming at us.

She slumped her shoulders as she turned and stared at me. "I just feel like we need to talk about it…" Her words trailed off. "About what happened. We never actually talked about how we felt that day. We just took it out on one another. We blamed one another for the accident, but we never actually talked about it."

We never really sat down at talked about it, she was right. We spent so much time thinking about how we felt and trying to pass the guilt on to one another. The only thing we discussed that didn't result in each of us turning on one another was her funeral. After that, all bets were off.

"We hadn't."

"I'm sorry for blaming you for what happened,"

Amanda said. "It wasn't your fault." She paced around the room, a dark cloud following her around, sucking all the joy from her.

It wasn't her fault either. "I wish every day that I would have told you, I was going to the back yard."

The reality was, we both left the yard at the same time for one reason or another, and neither of us told the other. That was what happened. We had a lapse in judgement, and we both paid the ultimate price for it. It was no one's fault. It just happened.

"I just wanted some explanation on why her. Why did it have to happen to her? She wasn't one to run into the street. What happened that day? What was going through her mind?"

Those thoughts crossed my mind one time or another. Ivory was always good for staying in the front yard and not running onto the road. But it still didn't change the fact that she was only three, almost four, and she was still a toddler with impulses.

"Maybe it's best to accept it was nothing but an unfortunate accident, Mandy."

She approached, and nestled her head into my chest. "It's just hard."

We hugged, as we relived the moment. It wasn't as numbing as those first few days, but there was an ache in my chest that constantly reminded me of that day. Instead of running from it, this time I was going to face it. I wasn't going to let grief steal me from my family again.

"I love you, Mandy."

Mandy flinched a bit, but didn't let go.

She pulled away after a few moments and took my

hands into hers. "Even when I was so mad at you, wanted to blame you for everything, I still loved you. Even when I told you I wanted a divorce. I just didn't know what to do, what to say to you?"

I took a step back and that guilt rushed over me. What did I do when she pulled the plug? I ran away like a coward. I ran to the first warm body that welcomed me with open arms. I threw my family away like trash instead of fighting for them. I was even lucky Amanda and I were in the same room.

Then she spoke again. "I just wish I would have tried a bit harder, you know. Instead of seeking comfort from someone who didn't give two shits about me, I wished I would have fought harder for our marriage."

Amanda was saying the same things I was feeling. Guilt. That was a good sign, right? That we were both acknowledging that we had shit all over our marriage, and we can finally stop blaming one another, so we can be a family like we had before. I know we could.

"We can't change what happened," I finally said. "But the question is, can we forgive and move on?"

It'd take time I knew, but if she could forgive and if we could let go of the resentment or at least try, then maybe we could make it. I didn't expect things to be the same, because they weren't. But it didn't mean we had to divorce.

"I forgive," Amanda said.

That was what I wanted to hear. I pulled her into a hug, sweeping her off her feet. I planted a soft kiss on her lips, before we naturally parted. A broad smile spread from cheek to cheek.

Amanda looked around the room. "We should

probably finish packing up all her things."

I nodded in agreement.

So, for the next hour, in silence, we packed up toys into boxes, and dragged them out to the living room. Amanda reached behind Ivory's bed and pulled out a custom made pink giraffe, with little pink bells hung around the giraffe's neck. She loved that thing, and wouldn't sleep without it. One time, I had driven across the city at 12 a.m., to give it to her, during a sleepover at Grandma's house.

"I'm going to keep this one." Amanda said. "We can give it to Joy. It'll be something from her big sister."

"Anything else you want to keep?" I asked.

She shook her head. "Everything else can go. Unless there is anything you want to keep."

I opted for the sketch book.

Soon, all that was left was the bed, an empty dresser and her desk and chair. It seemed so bittersweet. It was as if she never occupied this space. But it was time to let go. In the upcoming few weeks, I'd paint the room back to a neutral color. I closed the door to Ivory's former bedroom and walked into the hallway. Amanda was coming out of the nursery with Joy in hand.

"She was playing quietly like a big girl."

I pulled them both into a bear hug. I was lucky. I was a lucky man.

I naturally released them and followed them into the master bedroom. Amanda changed Joy. I sat on the bed beside her. Amanda sat Joy between the two of us. She was all smiles. I hoped to see more smiles and not to miss any more of her milestones going forward.

In the corner of my eye, under a stack of magazines,

the brown envelope containing the signed divorce papers stuck out. I hadn't gotten rid of them, and honestly, had forgotten about them. I stood from the couch, Amanda observed me. I retrieved the envelope.

She clenched her jaw.

"Where's the paper shredder?" I asked.

"Give them to me?" she said.

I handed them to her.

"Here, sit with Joy for a moment," she said. I replaced Amanda's spot on the bed.

She stared at the envelope, a look of aloofness. Then she sat on the bed, opened the flap. One by one she took each piece of paper, ripped it up and threw it. Then she did it to the next and the next. I had to keep Joy from eating the paper. Amanda didn't say a word, didn't make eye contact until the last page was in a pile of little pieces of paper.

"That is what I think of those." She chuckled. "Who needs a paper shredder?"

I laughed with her. My wife was back.

Amanda rose. "What do you say we get out of here? Maybe go see Ivory? All three of us? We can worry about all the stuff later."

"Okay"

We drove together, like a family, to the cemetery. Quietly, the three of us walked past the many tombstones until we reached where Ivory was laid to rest. I knelt on one side of the tombstone and Amanda the other, holding Joy.

"We're here, Ivory," I whispered.

Amanda ran her spare hand over the letters of her engraved name. "We'll see you on the other side, our baby girl."

Then we stood, letting Joy enjoy a moment with her sister in peace.